C000257711

DEATH ON THE WEST CLIFF

A KIPPER COTTAGE MYSTERY

JAN DURHAM

INKUBATOR
BOOKS

Published by Inkubator Books
www.inkubatorbooks.com

Copyright © 2023 by Jan Durham

ISBN (eBook): 978-1-83756-254-1
ISBN (Paperback): 978-1-83756-255-8
ISBN (Hardback): 978-1-83756-256-5

Jan Durham has asserted her right to be identified as the author of this work.

DEATH ON THE WEST CLIFF is a work of fiction. People, places, events, and situations are the product of the author's imagination. Any resemblance to actual persons, living or dead is entirely coincidental.

No part of this book may be reproduced, stored in any retrieval system, or transmitted by any means without the prior written permission of the publisher.

1

'N ot the real deal.' Skipper Masterson scratched his beard and turned his blue eyes to Liz McLuckie across their table in the Full Moon Café. 'Eleven letters. Fourth one N, last one T.'

'Tricky.' Liz leaned back and closed her own eyes, enjoying the warmth of the sunlight flooding in through the window. After the storms of the spring, summer seemed to be shaping up nicely in the little fishing town of Whitby. The Full Moon Café was warm and welcoming, with its assortment of mismatched tables, fairy lights and the delicious aroma of baking. Liz had to push through her general feeling of wellbeing to concentrate on the clue. She opened her eyes again as a thought occurred to her. '*Counterfeit*. How many letters does that have?'

Skipper counted. 'Eleven. It fits.' He scribbled it into the crossword with his ballpoint pen. 'You're not half bad at this.'

Liz smiled. 'What's the next one?'

'Six down. *Part of a kit*. Nine letters, starting with an s, sixth letter d, last letter m.'

'*Snaredrum*,' suggested Tilly, as she put Skipper's cheese toastie on the table in front of him. As usual she'd brought a waft of patchouli oil with her, and was dressed in an odd combination of clothes – a bandana over her bleach-blond hair, a Pink Floyd tee shirt and hotpants. She nodded at Liz's teapot. 'Do you want a top up?'

'No, thanks. I have to be going. I have to get this lot to the launderette.' She tapped the bag of laundry at her feet.

'You can't go yet.' Skipper finished scribbling Tilly's answer into the crossword. 'We're not even half way through.'

Liz laughed. 'Some of us have work to do.'

Skipper was, as his name suggested, the master of a fishing trawler based in the harbour. Usually at that time of the morning he would have just finished his shift at sea with his crew, but as the *Stella Mae* was currently having one of its winches repaired, he had the day off. An hour in the café was a luxury he was rarely able to enjoy.

'Sorry.' Liz stood up. She would have liked to stay longer and enjoy it with him, but it was changeover day for Kipper Cottage, and she had to get back before her new rental guest arrived. She picked up her bag of washing and called to her English bull terrier, who was snoozing in a patch of sunlight. 'Come on, Nelson.'

Nelson opened one piratically patched eye, sighed, then gave the plastic pig Tilly kept for him a goodbye squeeze. He trotted to join Liz as she headed for the door.

'Catch you later!' Tilly's wife Mags poked her head through the beaded curtain that led into the kitchen. Mags was as dark as Tilly was fair, as thoughtful as Tilly was impetuous. Yin to Tilly's Yang. They were the perfect couple. Liz nodded and blew her a kiss.

It was already busy outside on Sandgate. Tourist season was just getting underway, but already the narrow cobbled street was thick with day trippers peering into the windows of the little independent shops selling artisan jewellery, candy and antiques. In another week or so, once the school holidays began, the day trippers would be boosted by families heading to the fish restaurants for lunch or to the beach with their buckets and spades. Liz clipped Nelson onto his lead and took a deep breath of warm, salty air. She turned right, towards the town centre and the bridge over the harbour. Whitby was a town of two halves separated by water. The east side, where Liz lived, was the oldest part of town, a jumble of eighteenth century red-roofed fisherman's cottages linked by narrow alleyways, cobbled streets, and communal spaces known as yards. In the eighteenth century it had been home to thousands of seafaring folk – as many as two or three families to a cottage. Now it was a picturesque warren, beloved of tourists and photographers.

The west side was newer, built mainly in Regency and Victorian times. It was much more commercial, dominated by the West Cliff with its grand, pastel-coloured hotels overlooking the amusement arcades, souvenir shops, pubs and fish market on the quayside. The harbour separated the two sides of the town, and the only way across was the swing bridge.

When Liz and Nelson arrived at the eastern end of the bridge, the barriers were down and the bridge was open, allowing a yacht to pass through into the marina. They waited patiently with the other pedestrians for it to close again. Even though it was still early, Liz could already smell fish and chips, and see several huge herring gulls waiting hopefully for the fish shops to open. She could also see the

Stella Mae tied up on the quayside, riding on the swell of the tide. There was some activity on deck – mechanics repairing the winch. Skipper seemed to think it would only take the day and he'd be back out on the high seas that night.

The bell rang, and the bridge closed again. Liz hurried on, with Nelson trotting beside her. His coffin-shaped head was so large compared to his body that Liz always marvelled he could travel at any speed at all without pitching forward onto his nose. He was spectacularly unaerodynamic. Some unkind people had dubbed him the ugliest dog in Yorkshire, but every since the day Liz had spotted him in the rescue shelter, she had been his devoted fan, and he had been hers. He had, quite literally, saved her life.

They turned right at the end of the bridge and cut through the pedestrian walkway of St Ann's Staith to the quayside, past the fish market with its porthole windows and steel shutters. Then they walked along Pier Road, passing the amusement arcades, empty at that time of the morning but still flashing their lights and dinging their bells, hoping to lure someone inside. As Liz passed the fortune telling kiosk on the corner – *Fortunes told. Advice given* – she raised her hand to Rose Young, whom she could see sitting inside. Rose waved back.

Liz led Nelson up the stone steps cut into the steep West Cliff. She paused at the top, next to the whalebone arch, to get her breath back. The arch was a well-known Whitby landmark – the jawbone of a huge whale that had been erected on the West Cliff sometime in the mid-eighteen hundreds, as a memorial to all the whalers in the town who had died. The crumbling bone had been replaced at some point by a resin replica, but it remained a local beauty spot, framing the view of the ruined abbey and St Mary's church on the opposite cliff.

It took Liz a little longer to get her breath back than she expected. At fifty-one, she was reasonably fit and healthy, and – she liked to think – quite youthful looking. But sometimes she forgot she wasn't thirty years younger.

While she caught her breath, she and Nelson looked at the view. The little fishing town lay below them, glorious in the sunshine. Past the sheltering arms of its two piers, she could see the waves of the North Sea, crested with white. On the clifftop opposite stood the iconic ruins of Whitby Abbey, once a thriving Benedictine community, but now a gaunt reminder of the impermanence of power. Only the east wall remained fully standing with its hollow arched windows, a Gothic ruin than that had provided the inspiration for Bram Stoker's novel *Dracula*. From where Liz stood she could see the winding stone steps – all one hundred and ninety-nine of them – leading up to the abbey and the squat shape of St Mary's church on the clifftop.

Liz had moved to Whitby from Edinburgh six years before, after the death of her husband Mark. After four years in the town she realised she was still moving very slowly through the grieving process, and had looked around for something to keep her distracted and physically occupied. She'd taken on two rundown fisherman's cottages – Gull Cottage and Kipper Cottage – and had spent almost two years renovating them. It had been hard work, but immensely rewarding. She now lived in Gull Cottage with her young Irish lodger Niall, and rented Kipper out for holiday lets. It wasn't an easy way to earn a living, but it meant she was self-sufficient.

Which reminded her... she had to get to the launderette. She shouldered her bag of washing again.

'Come on, sweetie.'

Nelson gave her a resigned look, and got to his feet.

The Lost Sock launderette was tucked away in one of the back lanes behind Regent Crescent, but rather than heading to it directly, around the crescent, she walked along the promenade instead, from where she could look down onto the sandy beach that was already dotted with people, wind breakers and towels. She'd just passed the shelter where she sometimes liked to picnic, when she spotted a flash of blue light. She looked to see where it was coming from, and saw two police cars parked on Regent Crescent. Her heart skipped a beat. She thought at first they were parked beside the entrance to the Anchorage Retirement Home, where her friends Iris and Dickie lived, but then she realised they were actually several doors further along.

As if of their own accord, her feet turned towards the crescent. She cut through the car park and made a beeline across the grass, drawn to the strobing lights of the police cars like a moth to a flame.

As she got closer she could see the centre of activity was the West Cliff Gallery, which occupied the grandest building on the crescent. Liz had never ventured inside the gallery, intimidated by its grandeur and by the obvious quality of the paintings displayed in their windows.

She saw a figure she knew, standing beside one of the squad cars. Police Constable Williams's usually mournful features broke into a smile when he spotted her.

'Mrs Mac! How are you? I haven't seen you in a while.'

'I'm fine, thanks. I'm glad summer's here.' She was too curious to indulge in small talk. 'What's going on?'

PC Williams's long face assumed its habitual undertaker's expression. 'A bad business. A very bad business.'

Liz frowned. 'A break-in?'

He nodded. 'And worse.'

'Worse?'

They were interrupted by the appearance of an ambulance at the end of the crescent. It drove towards them without its lights on, and without sirens. Not a good sign.

PC Williams met her eyes. The young policeman gave a good impression of being a bit slow off the mark, but Liz knew he was a lot sharper than any of his colleagues gave him credit for. He'd seen Liz take note of the absence of lights and siren, and realise the significance.

'No one we know, I hope?' said Liz.

He just stared at her.

Liz took pity on him. 'It's okay. You don't have to tell me. I daresay I'll find out soon enough.'

'Actually,' he blurted, 'you *do* know him. Please don't tell anyone I told you, but it's Christian Petit.'

Liz stifled a cry of shock.

2

_____

'WHAT THE DEVIL WAS THE FRENCHIE DOING IN THERE ANYWAY? I THOUGHT HE WAS A FISHERMAN.' Iris Gladwell craned her neck to see out of her window, even though she knew perfectly well she wouldn't be able to see the gallery from where she was standing. She could, however, see the stationary ambulance, and subjected it to an interrogatory glare.

'He is,' said Liz. Then she corrected herself. 'He was. But maybe he was having trouble getting another job?'

'Pardon?' Dickie Ledgard leaned forward. 'I didn't quite catch that.' Dickie was deaf in one ear, the perfect companion for Iris, who never spoke at any volume less than a bellow. When Liz had first met her she'd thought the old lady was deaf herself, but it turned out she'd spoken like that all her life.

Iris addressed Dickie. 'SHE SAID MAYBE THE FRENCHMAN WAS STRUGGLING AFTER SKIPPER

FIRED HIM. I SUPPOSE HE WOULD, WITH THAT GAMMY LEG OF HIS.'

Dickie nodded.

'I CAN'T IMAGINE HIM WORKING IN A POSH PLACE LIKE THAT, THOUGH. OR MAYBE HE WASN'T WORKING THERE? MAYBE HE WAS THE ONE TRYING TO ROB IT!'

Liz was beginning to regret the impulse that had made her take refuge at the Anchorage Retirement Home. She'd just felt an urgent need to sit down for a bit, but had forgotten there would be a price to pay – Iris's inevitable curiosity. She hoped Iris would keep Christian Petit's demise to herself, at least until it was common knowledge. But she doubted it. She stood up.

'Thanks for the tea. I really have to go.' She still had her bag of laundry, and would barely have enough time to drop it at the laundrette and get back to Kipper Cottage before her guest, Mr Kep, arrived. He would have travelled a long way with his two dogs, and she didn't want him to find nobody at home.

Liz left Iris and Dickie to speculate about Christian Petit and headed to the launderette with Nelson. She dropped her laundry off then hurried back to the old town. When she reached the end of Henrietta Street she saw a figure with a suitcase and two cairn terriers standing outside Kipper Cottage. She hurried to join him.

'Mr Kep?' she gasped.

'Mrs McLuckie.' He shook her hand, while Nelson said a polite hello to the dogs.

'So sorry I'm late.'

'No worries. We've just got here, haven't we, girls?' he

addressed his terriers with an Australian accent. 'If you hadn't turned up we could have just gone for a little walkabout.'

Liz unlocked Kipper and showed him where everything was, including baskets and bowls for his dogs, Tammy and Cara. She was sure that one of the reasons Kipper Cottage was so popular with holidaymakers was because she was just as happy to take doggy guests as human ones. Possibly even more so. She left George Kep with a key and a reminder she was just next door if he needed anything.

Relieved to get home to Gull Cottage, she unclipped Nelson from his lead in the little kitchen and gave him his lunch, then climbed the steep wooden stairs to her sitting room and plopped down on the sofa. She was still in shock about Christian Petit. She had got to know him and his wife, Juliette, just a few months earlier, when one of Christian's fellow trawlermen had gone overboard in a storm. Shortly afterwards, Skipper had laid him off. The last time she'd seen Christian he'd been standing in his kitchen with his his baby daughter in his arms. Liz guessed that things had been tough for him and Juliette since he lost his job. She felt guilty she hadn't stayed in touch.

Her mobile rang, shattering her thoughts. It was Benedict. As always, her heart gave a little thump when she saw his name on caller ID.

'I've just heard about Christian Petit,' he said. News travelled fast in Whitby, and bad news fastest of all.

'How did you hear?'

'Iris. I just bumped into her in the café.'

'Ah.' So much for swearing the old lady to secrecy.

'Are you okay?'

'Yes. Just a bit shocked.'

'Apparently he'd recently started working as a night security guard in the gallery.'

'A bit different to fishing.'

'Just a bit.' He hesitated. 'Look, we're not particularly busy here. I could ask someone to step in for me, and come over if you want?' Benedict was head curator of the Captain Cook Maritime Museum. It was popular with tourists and she guessed he was stretching the truth when he said he wasn't busy. She was grateful for the offer, though. It gave her a warm feeling. When Mark had died she had genuinely thought that any chance of romance had died with him. Luckily, she'd been wrong.

'No, you're okay, thanks. I'm fine. It's not as if I knew Christian all that well.' In fact, she'd only met him for the first time a few months before, when she'd been looking into the death of one of his fellow fishermen, who had fallen overboard from the *Stella Mae*. 'I'm just a bit shaken, that's all.'

'Okay, if you're sure. You still on for dinner tonight?' he asked.

'Of course. Looking forward to it.'

'See you there at eight.'

Her phone rang again almost as soon as she hung up. She answered it.

'Kevin. How's things?'

'Not great. I'm tied up on the West Cliff. I don't suppose you fancy bringing me some lunch?'

Liz settled Nelson with a treat, then headed back to the West Cliff via the café. Everyone in the Full Moon was agog with the news of Christian's death, and, although no one knew any more details than she did, everyone seemed to have an opinion as to how he might have died. She was relieved when she was able to make her escape with her newly filled lunchbox.

When she got back up to the promenade she saw the police had erected a tent on the grass opposite the gallery. She settled herself in her favourite spot in the glass shelter on the clifftop, from where she had a good view of it all. She could see several forensic-suited figures coming in and out of the gallery and the tent. The squad cars had been moved further down the crescent, and Liz could see Kevin's car parked next to them. As she watched, a woman in a trouser suit with a sharp bob came out from the tent. Liz turned away quickly. She really didn't want Detective Inspector Flint to spot her. Luckily, Flint went straight into the gallery.

Finally, after about twenty minutes, she saw Kevin's familiar figure emerge from the gallery. He hurried across the grass, then crossed the road to join her in the shelter. Kevin was in his late twenties, with the freshly scrubbed look of an altarboy. She'd met the young Detective Sergeant shortly after her move to Whitby, and they'd become good friends, in spite of the age gap. Today he looked more than usually harassed – his cheeks were flushed and his tie was missing.

'Sorry to keep you waiting,' he said as he kissed her on the cheek. 'Hell of a nerve, when you've brought me lunch.'

'Don't be daft. I guessed you would have trouble getting away.' She opened her lunchbox. 'I have salmon sandwiches and your favourites – Tilly's sausage rolls.'

'You're a star.'

She poured them both a coffee from her flask while he attacked the food.

He saw she wasn't eating. 'Don't you want anything?' he asked, around a mouthful of salmon.

'I'm going out for dinner tonight. I'm saving myself.'

'Dinner with Dad?'

Liz nodded. She was so glad her romance with Benedict hadn't spoiled the easy-going relationship she and Kevin already enjoyed. It could very easily have been awkward.

Kevin swallowed his salmon. 'I have something I want to ask you.' He wiped his hands on his trousers, took a small velvet box from his pocket and opened it. An emerald-cut aquamarine flanked by diamonds flashed in the sunlight.

'I'm really flattered, Kevin, but...'

'Very funny.' He grinned at her. 'What do you think?'

'It's lovely. Really lovely. Is it Anna's size?'

Kevin nodded. 'I borrowed one of the rings from her jewellery box to make sure.'

Liz bit her lip. He might have 'borrowed' a ring Anna wore on a different finger, but she didn't want to spoil the moment by saying so. She also refrained from saying that Anna might have preferred to choose her own ring.

Kevin spotted her hesitation. 'Do you think it's too soon?' It was a valid question. He and Anna had only been dating about seven months, since they met over a cadaver in the police mortuary. He did seem to be moving very fast, but who was Liz to point that out? She shrugged instead.

'Only you and Anna can say, really.'

'What if I've misjudged it? What if she turns me down?'

'I suppose you won't know until you ask, will you? You just need to pick the right moment.'

Kevin scowled as he snapped the box shut and put it back in his pocket. 'I doubt that'll happen for days. Flint will have me working overtime.'

Liz saw her chance. 'Is it very bad?'

Kevin gave her a sideways look. He knew her too well. 'Bad enough.'

'You do know I know Christian... knew Christian... don't you? And his wife Juliette.'

Kevin sighed and capitulated. 'At the moment it's hard to tell what happened. There was a break-in, just after midnight. The alarm shows what time the power was cut.'

'They disabled the alarm?'

Kevin nodded. 'And the CCTV system. When the owner and his assistant opened the gallery this morning they found Christian dead at the bottom of the stairs.'

'Your dad says he was their security guard.'

Kevin nodded. 'Not a very good one, apparently.' He spotted Liz's expression. 'Sorry. '

'Do you think the burglars killed him?'

'That's the obvious conclusion to jump to, isn't it? But we still don't know how he died. We won't until they do the post mortem.'

'Was anything stolen?'

'We're not sure yet, but we don't think so. As far as James Bullington, the gallery owner, can tell, there's nothing missing.'

Liz frowned. The thieves had the run of the place. Why go to the bother of disabling the alarm and CCTV, and killing the security guard, if they weren't going to steal anything?

It was odd.

Liz took a detour on the way home to push a card through Juliette Petit's door. She'd thought long and hard about phoning her, before deciding not to. She hadn't really spoken to Juliette for weeks, and didn't want to look like some ghoulish ambulance chaser. The message she'd written on the card was short and to the point – she was sorry to hear about Christian and if Juliette wanted any help at all, she could call her. Liz guessed that with no family in the UK and a baby daughter to look after, Juliette would be feeling very alone.

She'd arranged to meet Benedict that evening at Whitby's most famous eatery, the Magpie Café. She was a little late, and when she turned the corner from St Ann's Staith she saw he was already waiting for her at the top of the entry steps. He kissed her as she joined him at the door.

'Sorry I'm late,' she said. 'I lost my phone again. Niall had to help me find it.'

Benedict grinned. 'I thought you'd stood me up."

'As if.' She kissed him back.

They went inside, where the warmth and bustle of the busy café wrapped round them like a hug. Liz took ages deciding what she wanted to eat from the menu. There was so much to choose from, all freshly prepared from the fish market on the quayside opposite. She finally decided on Magpie Medley – pan-fried halibut fillet, salmon, scallops and king prawns on Magpie potato hash with a creamy garlic sauce.

When they'd ordered, Benedict looked at her thoughtfully.

'We could have postponed, you know, if you weren't in the mood.' He ran a hand through his hair. The flashes of silver in it were the only thing that betrayed his fifty-something years, otherwise he was lean and athletic, almost boyish looking. They'd only been going out a few months, and he still had the power to make her heart skip a beat. It was a bit silly really, at her age.

'I'm fine. Honestly.'

'Still, it must have been a shock for you, about Christian Petit.'

'Not as much as it must have been for Juliette.' Liz wanted to change the subject. 'Have you spoken to Kevin lately?'

'Not since Mahjong last week. Why?'

Liz hesitated. Kevin hadn't sworn her to secrecy about the proposal, but... luckily, Benedict saw her hesitation and interpreted it correctly.

'He's told you he's going to propose to Anna?'

'Yes. He showed me the ring.'

'Pretty, isn't it?'

'It is.' She hesitated again.

'But?' Benedict scrutinised her face. 'I can sense a 'but'.'

'It's nothing, really... It's just, if it was me, I'd want to choose my own ring. It seems a bit old-fashioned to just spring one on her like that.'

'Really?'

Liz nodded. 'That's probably just me, though. The ring is beautiful.'

'Do you think we should throw them a surprise engagement party?'

Liz couldn't help her dismay from showing on her face. 'Maybe not a surprise one.'

Benedict's own expression clouded. 'You think she might turn him down?'

Liz shrugged. She really had no idea. Although Anna and Kevin had been going out for longer than she and Benedict had, she'd only met Anna half a dozen times. Anna's job as a coroner's assistant took up most of her time, and that, combined with Kevin's tricky shifts as a detective, meant there hadn't been much opportunity to get to know her.

She was saved from having to answer Benedict's question by the arrival of their dinner, fragrant and steaming, from the kitchen. Any thought of Kevin's impending nuptials was eclipsed by their appetites.

3

'It says here its worth about sixty thousand quid.' Niall tapped his copy of the *Whitby Bugle*.

'Really?' Liz sipped her tea.

Niall nodded and read aloud from the paper. '*The stolen portrait of Whitby noblewoman Lady Henrietta Cholmley by Sir Joshua Reynolds was expected to fetch in excess of sixty thousand pounds at auction later in the month.*'

'Very strange.' Liz frowned. 'Kevin said the gallery owner... Mr Wellington?'

'Bullington.'

'Mr Bullington didn't think there was anything missing. It's been more than a week since the break-in.'

'You'd think that would have been the first thing he checked, wouldn't you?' Niall's blue eyes widened as he put down the paper. 'If I had a painting worth sixty grand, I'd be straight in there, making sure it was okay.' He sneaked Nelson his last piece of sausage under the table.

Liz pretended not to see. She'd met Irishman Niall the

summer before, after he'd been fired from his archaeological dig at the abbey. They'd then both been caught up in a sensational murder investigation that had almost ended in tragedy. After that he'd become a permanent fixture at Gull Cottage, helping her out with her renovations and chores in lieu of rent. In spite of the age gap – Niall was in his early twenties – Liz had become very fond of him, and liked to think the feeling was mutual.

He drained his mug and stood up. 'Got to dash, or I'll be late.' He'd recently changed careers from archaeology to acting, and was attending college in Middlesbrough. 'You in tonight, or out?'

'Out. Benedict's taking me to the theatre in York.'

'Nice.' He headed for the door. 'Oh, I forgot to ask. We don't have ghosts, do we?'

'Ghosts?' Liz saw his expression and realised he wasn't being serious. 'I don't think so. Why?'

'I heard some strange noises this morning. They sounded like they were coming from the sitting room.'

'Really? What kind of noises?'

'A kind of scratching sound. Could have been the wind, or mice, I suppose.'

'Maybe,' she said doubtfully. It was a calm morning, not particularly windy, and she hadn't seen any evidence of mice lately.

After Niall had gone, Liz went up to the sitting room to take a look. There was no sign of anything that might have caused the noises. Everything was as it should be in the small, beamed room, with its inglenook fireplace and the sun streaming through the window onto her battered Chesterfield sofa. She would have liked to curl up there with a book, but instead she went back downstairs to tidy up the breakfast things, then she took Nelson for his morning walk.

They went up the one hundred and ninety-nine steps that led to the ruined Benedictine abbey on the clifftop and the graveyard of St Mary's church. It was Nelson's favourite spot to chase rabbits, although he'd never actually managed to catch one. It didn't stop him trying, though. While he was dodging frantically between the ancient leaning gravestones, Liz did a slow lap of St Mary's church, breathing in the fresh salt air that blew in off the North Sea. Then they headed back down the steps.

When they reached the bottom they saw a familiar red-faced figure in a high-viz jacket, pulling a trolley of herring to the smokehouse in Henrietta Street. Mike Howson owned a popular wet fish shop on Baxtergate, on the other side of the harbour, where he also lived with his wife and two sons.

'Ay up, Mrs Mac.' He bent to give Nelson a scratch behind the ears. 'Wotcha, Nelson.'

'How're things, Mike?' Mike was Liz's chief source of news in the town. He seemed to know everyone, and, although he would have been offended to be called a gossip, he *loved* to talk. Liz knew it wouldn't take him long to fill her in on the latest news.

'Terrible business up on the West Cliff, eh?' Mike rubbed one of his red cheeks.

'Terrible,' agreed Liz.

'Did you know the French lad at all?'

Liz nodded.

'A solid family man, from what I saw. But his wife's going to be struggling now. I've heard the gallery has no insurance on him, because he was technically self-employed.'

'Poor Juliette.' Liz still hadn't seen or heard from Juliette since his death, and was starting to feel guilty about it.

'That isn't the worst of it, either,' continued Mike. She could tell from the gleam in his eyes he had something particularly juicy to share.

'Oh?'

'That James Bullington is throwing a swanky party at the gallery tonight.' Mike saw Liz's astonishment. 'He's tried to keep it quiet, but... it beggars belief, with the lad not even buried yet.'

Liz had to agree. She could maybe see the rationale behind it – Bullington still had his gallery to run and must have been keen to signal it was business as usual – but it still seemed incredibly insensitive under the circumstances.

JULIETTE PETIT LIVED in one of the blocks of flats on the east quay, at the far end of Church Street. Built sometime in the thirties or forties, it was accessed by staircases and balconies at the back. There were no signs of life when Liz knocked at the door of her flat – the curtains were drawn and everything was quiet. Liz knocked a couple of times before turning to make her way back down the staircase. Pricked by guilt, she had decided to call on Juliette after her chat with Mike, but had to admit to herself that she was relieved to find no one at home.

But then she heard the door open behind her. She turned to see Juliette's pale face peeking out. She spotted Liz.

'Oh, it's you,' she muttered, without enthusiasm.

Liz retraced her steps back up the stairs with reluctant feet. 'I thought I'd come and see if you needed anything.'

'I need nothing. Apart from my husband.'

'I'm so sorry, Juliette. I would have come sooner, only...' Liz tailed off, not knowing how to finish the sentence.

'I suppose you should come in.' Juliette opened the door to show Liz inside.

The flat still had no carpets, and only the bare minimum of furniture. Liz looked around for Juliette's baby girl, and saw her asleep in a buggy in the corner, jam smeared on her mouth.

'How are you getting on?' asked Liz in hushed tones, even though she already knew the answer. Juliette looked nothing like her usual elegant self. Her long blond hair was scraped into a greasy ponytail, and, free of make-up, she looked like an exhausted snail without its shell.

'I am managing.' Juliette gave an entirely gallic shrug. 'As soon as the police release Christian's body I am taking him to his family in Limoges.'

'Are you coming back? To Whitby?'

'*Pourquoi*? There is nothing for me here. This town has hardly taken me to its bosom.' That was true, but it was at least partly due to Juliette's prickly, standoffish nature. As an incomer herself, Liz hadn't found it easy to integrate in the town at first. Many of the residents had been born and raised there, and everyone knew each other, but with a little bit of effort and an open heart she'd soon made friends – good friends – and now regarded Whitby as her home.

Juliette sniffed. 'It is all Skipper's fault.'

Liz stared at her, dismayed.

'If he had not fired Christian from the *Stella Mae* for no reason, Christian would not have struggled to get another job. It was not easy, you know, because of his leg.' Christian walked with a limp, the result of a car accident when he was younger. It hadn't seemed to bother him on board, but was quite pronounced on dry land. Juliette continued. 'If it wasn't for Skipper, Christian would never have had to take that terrible job in the art gallery.'

That was true. But Skipper *had* had a compelling reason for making Christian redundant, one he felt bad about but couldn't explain to anyone. Liz's investigation into the death on the *Stella Mae* hadn't ended with the usual revelation and arrest of the guilty party – it had resulted in a secret that needed to be kept. If Christian had remained as part of Skipper's crew, he would have been uncomfortably close to uncovering it. Skipper had had no choice but to make him redundant. But of course, Liz couldn't tell any of that to Juliette.

Juliette continued, oblivious. 'Skipper is as bad as that terrible man Bullington. You have heard, I suppose, that he is having a party at the gallery tonight?'

Liz hesitated. She didn't want to make Juliette even angrier.

'A party! When my Christian is still in the mortuary. It is... disgraceful... *irrespectueux!*'

'It is. I agree.'

'Skipper and Bullington are as bad as each other.'

'They didn't kill Christian, Juliette.'

As Juliette looked at Liz, her eyes filled with tears. She put her hands over her face, overcome. Liz put her arms around her awkwardly until her sobs subsided. Grief was a terrible thing. Even now, more than five years after Mark's death, Liz was still ambushed by it sometimes. It would pounce on her when she was least expecting it, tearing and ripping. She knew Juliette had a very long way to go.

Juliette straightened up suddenly in her arms. 'But I was

forgetting!' she exclaimed, wiping her face with her hand. 'You are a detective, *non*?'

'No.' Liz grimaced. 'Not really.'

'Oh, but you are! You solved that case up at the museum. And found the person who killed the mayor.' Juliette's eyes swam with hope. 'You can find whoever killed my poor Christian.'

'The police are working on it.'

'Pfft. The police. That horrible woman, Flint. She is only interested in making people feel small.' Juliette's gaze narrowed. 'You will help me find the killer?'

'I would if I could, only...' Liz chose her words carefully. 'Inspector Flint has said she'll arrest me if I get involved in police work again.' She knew that threat wasn't an idle one.

'I did not take you for a coward, Liz.'

'I'm sorry.'

'Go, THEN!' Juliette pointed dramatically at the door. 'I will do it on my own. Masterson, Bullington, and whoever killed him. I will make them all pay.'

'Did you know there's a party at the West Cliff Gallery tonight?' asked Liz.

Benedict nodded. 'I was invited.' He saw her puzzled expression. 'Not personally, but Connie asked me to go as her plus one.'

Constance Threadwell was an old college friend of Benedict's, who was responsible for the northern division of Sotheby's. She and Benedict met up occasionally for a coffee or a drink whenever she was up from London. Liz had never met her.

'I told her I couldn't go because we had tickets for the theatre,' added Benedict.

'Oh.'

They were sitting in his tiny office at the Captain Cook Memorial Museum in Grape Lane, a narrow building four storeys high, criss-crossed with wooden beams and filled with sea-faring exhibits. As an ex-navy man and expert on maritime antiques, Benedict was the perfect curator.

'You do still want to go, don't you?' he asked. 'To the theatre?'

'Of course.'

But he'd seen her hesitation. He looked at her quizzically.

'I've just been to see Juliette,' she said.

'Oh?' Benedict frowned, clearly trying to work out what that might have to do with their proposed theatre visit.

'Mmm. She's in a bad way.'

'Hardly surprising.' His frown deepened, still no wiser about where the conversation was headed.

'She asked if I could help her find Christian's killer.'

'Ah.' His brow cleared. 'Isn't that a bit out of your league?'

'Is it?' She tried and failed to keep the sharpness from her voice. She had, after all, been instrumental in catching several murderers, and, most recently, in unmasking another two, although no one in the town was aware of that, not even Benedict.

'You know what I mean,' Benedict rushed to smooth her ruffled feathers. 'The police are all over this. Kevin says they already have a couple of suspects.'

'Did he say who?'

'No.' He hesitated. 'Although he did tell me that Flint also has Tilly in her sights again.'

Liz sighed. When Tilly was younger she'd done time in a juvenile facility for breaking and entering, a fact that Detective Inspector Flint used as an excuse to harass her at every opportunity. Flint seemed determined to arrest Tilly for something, and Liz suspected that was at least partly due to Tilly's friendship with Liz.

'All the more reason for me to go to this party, don't you think?' she said.

'You?' Benedict was startled.

'If I find whoever broke into the gallery, then Tilly will be in the clear. Also, I feel really bad for refusing to help Juliette. She thinks the whole town is against her.'

Benedict said nothing.

'She's all on her own now, with her baby daughter to look after.'

Still nothing from Benedict.

Liz ploughed on. 'I would quite like to go to this party, if I can get an invite.' She paused. 'Do you think Constance might take me?'

'I've already turned her down because *we* were supposed to be going to the theatre.'

'She wouldn't hold that against you, surely?'

Benedict looked peeved, and Liz couldn't really blame him. She supposed it was a bit of a cheek. Finally, he spoke. 'Okay. If that's what you want, I'll ask her.'

'We can go to the theatre another time.'

Benedict nodded. 'It's okay.' But Liz saw the left hand corner of his mouth flicker, almost imperceptibly. Benedict had a tell that she'd come to recognise during their many evenings playing Mahjong. Whenever he bluffed, or told a lie, the left hand corner of his mouth would twitch. It was a dead giveaway, and one he was entirely unable to control, even though she'd warned him about it.

She hated to upset Benedict, but if the party was an opportunity to find out something about Christian Petit's killer, it was a price she was prepared to pay.

She would make it up to Benedict later.

4

'There's definitely something up there,' muttered Niall, peering into the blackness of the sitting room chimney. 'I can hear it.'

'Oh no. Poor thing.' Liz leaned in for a better look, but couldn't kneel down because she was wearing her best skirt, and there was quite a lot of soot in the hearth. It was clear, however, that they had discovered their ghost – or at least the source of the noises Niall had heard that morning.

'It might die up there if we don't get it out,' said Niall.

'I'll go and get changed. It doesn't matter if I'm a bit late.'

She'd spent the best part of an hour getting ready for the gallery party, carefully taming her curls and making up her face. She didn't consider herself a particularly vain person but knew she brushed up pretty well. Although her curly chestnut hair was her only real claim to beauty, she looked younger than her age and her figure wasn't in bad shape, in spite of her aversion to exercise. She had chosen her outfit for the night with care – a silky skirt and a cream lace shirt that showed a bit of cleavage but not too much. She'd also decided to wear heels, even though she was finding that increasingly difficult. She tried not to wonder why she was making so much effort but guessed deep down that it was because she was going to be meeting Constance for the first time. A smidge of rivalry there?

She changed back into her jeans and rejoined Niall in the sitting room.

'Thanks,' he said. 'It is probably easier with two of us. We can't leave it up there.'

They both stared up into the chimney. Although Liz had heard some scratching and fluttering earlier, everything was quiet now.

'Perhaps it's died,' she said.

'Or maybe it's just exhausted. I could go up onto the roof. I might be able to see it better from there.'

Liz didn't like the sound of that. 'Let's see what we can do from down here first. Go and get the broom from downstairs, will you?'

While Niall was gone she climbed further into the hearth and peered up the chimney again. It was completely black, when she should have been able to see the sky, metres above her. It was so dark, however, that it was impossible to see exactly where the bird had lodged itself.

'Here you go.'

Liz took the broom and slowly pushed the handle up the chimney, trying to ignore the dirt she could feel pattering down onto her face. 'I can't feel anything. It must be too far up.'

'I have a longer reach than you. Let me have a go.'

They swapped places. Liz gave him the broom.

After a moment or two of prodding, he spoke excitedly. 'I

can feel something.' They were rewarded with a rustling noise. 'It's still alive.'

'Gently. We don't want to hurt it.'

Niall withdrew the broom handle and looked at her, his face flecked with soot. Liz knew hers must be the same. 'What now?' he asked.

Suddenly there was a whooshing sound, and Niall only just managed to pull back in time before something black and spiky landed with a thump on the hearth. It was motionless for a moment, then burst up into the air towards them. It bounced off Niall, then away again, ricocheting around the walls – a frightened ball of feathers and soot, smearing black.

'Open the window!' shouted Niall. He corralled the bird – it was impossible to tell what kind it was – into a corner as Liz rushed to open the window. Together they shepherded it towards the open casement. Eventually it flapped up and out, but not before it had daubed the whole room generously with smut.

'Oh my God,' breathed Liz, gazing around. 'What a mess.'

Niall wiped his face with his forearm. 'Sure, but don't you worry about that. Go and sort yourself out for your party. I'll clean up in here.'

LIZ SIPPED HER CHAMPAGNE COCKTAIL, letting the sound of chatter and music – jazz lite – wash over her. She was standing awkwardly in a corner of the gallery, watching the other party guests mingle, surreptitiously trying to scrape soot from under her fingernails. On the other side of the room she could see Constance chatting to a tall, dapper-

looking gent in a pale suit. Liz guessed he was the owner of
the gallery, James Bullington. Constance had been surprised
by Benedict's request to take Liz to the party instead of him.
Liz suspected she wasn't at all happy with the substitution
but had been too well-mannered to refuse. She wasn't at all
what Liz had expected – tall, with pale, patrician features.
Her glossy brunette hair brushed her bare shoulders above a
black cocktail dress. From everything Benedict had said of
Constance's art history expertise and dedication to her job,
Liz had expected someone much more academic looking.
Much more... frumpy... if she was honest. She wasn't at all
sure she was happy with the discrepancy.

'Hello! Have you had a look around yet?' A young man
with freckles and orange hair approached her.

'Um... no. Not yet.'

'I don't think we've met.' He held out his hand for Liz to
shake. 'I'm Brian, James's gallery assistant.'

'Liz.'

'From?'

'From nowhere really. I'm Constance's plus one.'

To his credit, Brian managed to hide his surprise pretty
well. He grinned. 'In that case I should give you the star
treatment. Would you like a tour?'

'Yes, please.'

They started upstairs, in what had originally been the
first floor drawing room, where several large modern paintings and sculptures were displayed. The architectural bones
of the Regency house had been retained, and the original
fireplace and cornicing were a surprisingly effective comple-
ment to the cleverly lit art. Brian was an attentive guide. He
realised pretty quickly that she was no art expert and
happily dumbed-down his explanations, without conde-

scension, while Liz asked the occasional question she hoped wasn't too silly. After the drawing room they toured the smaller rooms upstairs, where there was some photography, and some mid-century abstracts. Then they went downstairs.

Brian led her into the smaller back room, where the centrepiece was a small portrait, displayed on an easel.

'This is the star of our collection at the moment.'

A languid lady leant against a balustrade in a bucolic landscape, draped in a loose gown trimmed with ermine, with pearls at her throat. Her hair hung artfully over one shoulder as she gazed into the distance. She reminded Liz a little of Constance... and also rang another bell. As uneducated as she was, she recognised the painting style.

'That's not...?' she began.

'By Sir Joshua Reynolds, yes. Lady Henrietta Catherine Cholmley. One of the famous Whitby Cholmleys.'

'But... I thought this had been stolen?'

Brian pulled a face. 'We have no idea where the *Bugle* got that story. They probably heard about the break-in, knew we had the Reynolds here and jumped to conclusions.'

'So the burglars didn't take anything?' she said.

'Nothing at all.'

'Come, come, Brian. Let's not bore our guests with that dreary tale.' James Bullington smiled down at Liz with very white teeth. With his overly black hair and smooth tanned skin, it was difficult to tell how old he was. Liz guessed he was considerably older than he liked to present himself. Older, certainly, than she was. 'Your glass is empty, my dear. Come and get a refill.'

He took her elbow and steered her back into the main

reception room. Brian followed as James replaced Liz's empty glass with a fresh one from the drinks table.

'Tell me how you know dear Connie.'

Liz was about to give him an answer she hoped was suitably vague, when she was distracted by an unexpected growling noise. She saw it came from a pekinese dog sitting in an ornate tented dog bed beside the drinks table. Its bulging black eyes were fixed ferociously on her.

'Behave yourself, Mr Dandy.' James wagged a finger at the dog. 'I don't know what's got into him.'

'Maybe he can smell my bull terrier,' suggested Liz.

As if to confirm her words, the pekinese jumped out of his bed and darted towards her, yipping and snarling.

'Mr Dandy! Behave!' scolded Bullington.

But Mr Dandy didn't behave. He did just the opposite, darting forward and nipping Liz's ankle with his tiny teeth.

'Ow!' Liz couldn't help her exclamation. She clapped her hand to her ankle.

'Brian! Brian!' shouted Bullington. 'Come and do something about Mr Dandy.'

Brian appeared as if by magic and scooped up the bundle of angry fur. 'I'll put him in the utility room.' He hurried off with his still-bristling burden.

'Is everything okay?' Constance glided over to them. 'Are you okay, Elizabeth?'

'Liz... Yes, thank you, Constance. I'm fine.'

But she wasn't fine. She was mortified that the conversation in the room had stopped and everyone was staring. The last thing she'd wanted was to draw attention to herself. What was supposed to have been a discreet information-gathering operation had turned into a spectacle.

Constance turned to Bullington and put a manicured

hand on his sleeve. 'I'm so sorry, James, for causing such a fracas.'

'Don't fret, Constance, dear. Mr Dandy will be fine, I'm sure.'

They both seemed oblivious to the fact that Liz was actually bleeding. A thin line of blood was trickling from the nick on her ankle into her shoe.

Brian spotted it as he rejoined them. 'Can I get you a plaster?'

'It's nothing, really. I'm sure it'll be okay in a minute.' She tried to ignore it, hoping that everyone else would do the same. Brian steered her away from Bullington and Constance.

'Sorry about Mr Dandy. James insists on bringing him into work, but he's a bloody nightmare.' He hesitated. 'Please don't tell him I said that.'

'I think Mr Dandy is probably aware of his bad behaviour.'

Brian grinned.

At that moment, the bell on the glass door to the foyer gave a discreet *bing-bong*, and a dishevelled figure pushed its way in, carrying a bucket. Liz stared aghast at Juliette. The French woman turned her savage gaze around the room. She put down her bucket and put her hands on her hips, glaring at them all. It took a moment or two for the chatter to die down, as people turned to look at her. James Bullington frowned.

'Are you all enjoying yourselves?' demanded Juliette. 'Are you enjoying your *Masque of the Red Death*? Don't you know me, *Monsieur* Bullington?'

It was clear from his expression that James was struggling to place her.

Liz got the reference to the *Masque of the Red Death*, and felt a twinge of guilt. She shouldn't be there.

Juliette lifted her chin and addressed Bullington. 'I am the woman you made a widow, not two weeks ago. And yet here you all are, laughing and drinking as if nothing has happened. As if my poor Christian hadn't died.'

James stepped towards her. 'Mrs Petit, we feel for your loss, we really do, but–'

Juliette didn't wait for him to finish, but picked up her bucket and heaved it at him. Everyone exclaimed as he was doused in red liquid that looked alarmingly like blood.

Juliette surveyed her handiwork with satisfaction. '*Et voila*! Now your outside resembles your inside.'

'Don't just stand there, Brian!' James Bullington spluttered through the liquid streaming down his face. 'Get her!'

Brian's expression betrayed his dismay, but, ever game, he ran towards Juliette. She evaded him and darted back out the door. Brian didn't follow. He clearly thought it was above his pay grade to chase her through the streets.

'You all saw that!' sputtered James Bullington, wiping his face. 'You saw what she did!'

Constance put a soothing hand on his arm. She'd been standing the closest to him, and had red splashes on her arms and shoulders. 'Don't worry. The police will find her.'

'The paintings,' gasped James. 'Are they okay?'

Brian did a quick triage. 'I think so. Apart from the Cornish.' Miraculously, all the paintings had escaped the deluge except one, a small landscape displayed on an easel that had been peripherally in Juliette's line of fire.

Constance took charge. 'James, why don't you go upstairs and get changed. I'll take care of the Cornish. Brian, can you get me some paper towels, please?'

Brian and James disappeared into the back room, while the rest of the guests clotted in groups to speculate about what had happened. By the level of the noise, Liz guessed it had been the most entertaining gallery event they'd attended in a while.

She joined Constance at the easel. The landscape in question was a beach scene, quite impressionistic, with two small figures – children – playing in a rock pool at the water's edge. It was streaked with red.

Constance rubbed at her arms.

'Are you okay?' asked Liz. 'I hope none of that went on your dress.'

'I'm sure it's fine.' Constance smiled at her brightly. 'Did you know you have a black mark on your chin?'

Liz blinked. Soot? She wiped her chin surreptitiously with her hand, embarrassed and angry. Had it been there all evening? Why hadn't Constance mentioned it sooner?

Brian reappeared with a roll of kitchen paper. 'Here you go.' He gave it to Constance, who tore off a sheet and started to dab it expertly on the landscape.

'I think it's just dyed water. Very dilute. It will come off the oil no problem.' She continued to dab, then paused. 'Oh.'

'What?' asked Brian, alarmed by her tone.

Constance stared at the paper towel in her hand. It was pink from Juliette's concoction, but had other colours on it too – blue and grey. Constance frowned up at the gallery assistant. 'I'm so sorry, Brian, but this painting... it's a fake.'

5

'What are you doing here?' As soon as he spotted Liz among the guests, Kevin led her discreetly away from the others, into the foyer.

'I was invited.'

'Is that Connie in there too?'

'Yes. You know her then?'

'Of course I do. She and Dad have been mates for years.'

Liz tried to hide her irritation. She couldn't imagine Constance Threadwell being a 'mate' to anyone, except in the biological sense, and she *really* didn't want to think about that.

'Liz!' Kevin broke into her train of thought.

'Mm?'

'This isn't good. Flint's on her way. When we go back in, hide behind the others and hope she doesn't notice you. With a bit of luck she won't spot you on the guest list either.'

But Liz wasn't listening. She was distracted by the staircase leading to the first floor, and – more particularly – by the floor immediately under the curving balustrade.

'Is that where you found Christian?' she asked.

'What?' Kevin ran a hand through his hair – a gesture that reminded her of his father – and followed the direction of her gaze. 'Yes, it is.'

Liz stared at the floor. There was no sign of Christian or his demise now – the marble tiles were as pristine there as they were everywhere else.

Kevin rolled his eyes. 'Oh, for heaven's sake. Go back in, and do your best to blend into the background. Okay?'

'Okay.'

She only just made it in time before Detective Inspector Flint arrived. Flint looked deceptively cool, with her sleek bobbed hair and expensive skirt suit, her elegance only slightly undermined by her neon trainers. She soon took charge, taking the main players – Bullington, Constance and Brian – to one side to question them.

'It was definitely Juliette Petit?' Liz heard her ask.

Kevin was taking the name and contact details of all the other guests present, so they could make a statement later if necessary. Liz hung around with the other bit-players, while being careful to stay in earshot of the main stage.

'I said so, didn't I?' snapped Bullington. 'On the telephone call. What are you even here for? You should be arresting her.'

'You want to press charges?'

'Of course I do. She's damaged a valuable painting.'

Liz suspected Bullington's outrage was more to do with Juliette humiliating him in front of his guests.

'Actually, James, the Cornish isn't at all valuable,' cut in Constance.

'That's neither here nor there, is it?' said Bullington. 'The point is, it *could* have been.'

'I'm sorry.' Irritation laced Flint's voice. 'What are you talking about?'

'The landscape that had paint thrown on it. *The Rockpool* by Norman Cornish,' explained Constance. 'It was supposedly painted in nineteen thirty-nine, but I doubt this version is more than three weeks old.'

'You're saying it's a fake?' asked Flint. 'Did you know that, Mr Bullington?'

'Of course not,' snapped Bullington. 'I'm not in the habit of selling fake art.'

'How much is it worth?'

'About eighteen thousand pounds.' It was Constance who answered Flint's question. 'If it was put into a good auction house. If it was authentic.'

Bullington interrupted testily. 'Aren't we getting off the point here? You need to arrest Mrs Petit.'

'Her husband's just died,' said Flint. 'Are you sure you want me to do that?'

With that one question, Flint went up massively in Liz's estimation.

Bullington, however, wasn't impressed. 'Good God, woman. Don't you think I know that better than anyone?'

'And yet you threw a party? Here? I can arrest Mrs Petit for criminal damage, but the charge is–' Flint broke off.

Liz looked up from the floor, to which she had apparently been giving her full attention, and flinched as her eyes met the Detective Inspector's. She'd been so intent on the conversation that she hadn't realised most of the other guests had been allowed to go. Their absence had left her unwittingly exposed.

Flint scowled and finished what she was saying. 'The charge is unlikely to stick, Mr Bullington. Which wouldn't look good for any of us.'

Liz almost snorted. She'd thought for a moment that Flint had a heart, but she should have known better.

'We have witnesses,' continued Bullington. 'I want her arrested.'

Flint shrugged. 'If you're sure.'

Liz took the opportunity to sidle towards the door.

'Mrs McLuckie!' Flint strode towards her, putting herself between Liz and the door. 'What are you doing here?'

'I was invited.'

'Really?'

'Really. You can ask Mr Bullington.'

'I will.' Flint turned away from Liz. 'Ossett, be sure to get this woman's name and address.'

Kevin, who had just finished taking the last guest's details, blinked at Flint, baffled. They all knew Liz and where she lived.

'Did you hear me, Ossett?'

'Yes, ma'am.'

Flint returned to Constance and James Bullington without looking at Liz again.

'I told you to stay out of sight,' hissed Kevin as she joined him. 'Or have you forgotten what happened last time?'

She could hardly forget. After failing to heed Flint's warning to steer clear of the police investigation into the deaths at the Anchorage Retirement Home, she'd spent several hours in a police cell. Even though she'd eventually been released, it was an experience she wasn't keen to repeat. If she was going to help Juliette she would have to be a lot more careful.

As Kevin made a show of writing down her name and address in his book, something occurred to Liz.

'Isn't this kind of thing below your pay grade?' she asked.

'Given Petit's death and the high profile of some of the guests, the Super wanted to involve as few people as possible. I've called Dad to let him know what's going on. He's asked you and Constance to go back to his house when we're done.'

'THANK YOU SO MUCH, B, for offering to put me up for the night.' Constance curled her long legs under her on the sofa and leaned back. 'I'm utterly exhausted.' Delilah, Benedict's oldest cat, jumped onto her lap.

'It was the least I could do, Con.' Benedict turned to Liz with a smile. 'How's the hot chocolate?'

'Lovely.' Liz sipped at the mug with a scowl. Benedict gave her a searching look, before turning back to Constance.

'I don't think I've ever heard of Norman Cornish,' he said.

'He's very collectable. *The Rockpool* is an unusual work for him, though. He didn't usually paint in oils, or do landscapes. He preferred people, ordinary people going about their business in mining communities.'

'Sounds right up my street,' said Benedict.

'They have a collection at the University of Northumbria. I'll take you there some time.'

Deciding Constance had held the stage for long enough, Liz chipped in. 'Do you think Bullington had any idea the painting was a fake?'

Constance shook her head. 'I shouldn't think so. It was a

very, very good fake. James was devastated. Hardly surprising, seeing as he owns it.'

'Owns it?' echoed Liz.

'Part of it. He inherited it with his sisters when his mother died last year. He was talking to me about putting it in the next London auction.'

'You think he'd have got eighteen thousand for it?'

'At least. The mining artists are very popular with Russian collectors.' Constance yawned and stretched theatrically, then looked at her watch.

Liz took the hint. She finished her hot chocolate and got to her feet. 'I should get off home.'

Benedict stood up too. 'Really?'

'It is quite late.'

'Goodnight, Elizabeth.' Constance stroked Delilah, who was purring. Liz suffered a stab of jealousy – the elderly cat never came anywhere near her, probably because she could smell Nelson.

''Night, Constance.'

Benedict followed Liz into the hallway. He kissed her.

'Are you sure you won't stay over?' he asked.

So far Liz had never slept at Benedict's house. She'd never really felt comfortable enough to do it – it was too full of memories of his dead wife Katherine, too full of her things, too full of her cats. Constance clearly had no such qualms.

'I don't think this is the right time; do you?' said Liz.

'No, you're probably right. But let me walk you home at least?'

'I'll be fine. Stay and look after your guest.'

'Con will be okay. She's a big girl.'

'So am I. I think I can get myself home.'

'If you're sure.' He kissed her goodnight.

Liz walked home slowly. It was a calm summer night, with only a few people out and about on the streets. The moon glinted off the water of the harbour as she crossed the swing bridge. Rather than head straight home along Church Street, she took off her heels and cut across Tate Hill beach, enjoying the sensation of the pebbles under her aching feet, and soothed by the sound of the waves. She tried not to think too hard about Constance and Benedict alone together, and failed. Was she imagining things, or did Constance have designs on Benedict? They'd known each other a long time; surely Constance would have made her move by now? But then Liz remembered it was still only eighteen months since Katherine had died. Perhaps Constance had been waiting a respectable amount of time before trying to upgrade her friendship with Benedict?

'Gah!' Liz kicked a pebble painfully into the sea, and shoved Constance – and Katherine – out of her head.

She thought instead about the scene at the gallery. The paint stunt was a shocking thing for Juliette to do, but Liz really couldn't blame her. The party had been callous, so soon after Christian's death. Had Juliette been arrested? Liz hoped that Flint was right, and that the charge wasn't likely to stick. Under the circumstances, Juliette might get off with a warning. There had been no real damage done, except to Bullington's pride.

The painting was hardly Juliette's fault. If it had been genuine it never would have smeared when Constance tried to clean it. It could easily have gone undetected until it went to auction. Liz wondered. Could the fake painting have anything to do with the break-in? The thieves hadn't stolen the Reynolds portrait, as the *Bugle* claimed – they hadn't

taken anything at all. Might they have swapped the real
Rockpool for the fake?

If so, why? Why go to all the trouble of breaking in and
killing Christian for a painting that was only worth eighteen
thousand pounds? It was a fair amount of money, but
nowhere near as much as the Reynolds was worth. Why
hadn't the burglars taken that? Why would they bother
swapping *The Rockpool* for a copy, when they could have just
taken it?

It didn't make any sense.

6

Liz lay in her bed under the eaves of Gull Cottage and listened to the rain. She'd been woken by the sound of St Mary's church bell striking six o'clock on the cliff top above her, and knew it wouldn't be long before Nelson woke up too. She snuggled under the duvet, wanting that moment of blissful comfort to last as long as possible. She'd woken up feeling deflated. Was it the scene with poor Juliette the night before? Or the thought of Constance waking up in Benedict's house? There was no doubt that Constance had disturbed her equilibrium. She hadn't expected her to be so attractive, but was her own self-esteem so low that she couldn't handle some competition? Perhaps it had knocked her sideways because she hadn't felt quite so close to Benedict since the affair at the Anchorage Retirement Home, when she'd investigated the mysterious deaths of two of the elderly tenants. She gave herself a mental shake – lying in her bed stewing about it wouldn't do anyone any good.

She swung her legs out of bed and dressed quickly.

. . .

IT WAS STILL RAINING when she and Nelson got to the top of
the abbey steps. She'd stopped as usual to look at the view
from one of the coffin steps half way up – so called because
they were wider, to give pall bearers somewhere to rest on
their way up to the church – but the low cloud made it
impossible to see much more than the red-tiled roofs of the
cottages immediately below. She pulled her raincoat tighter
around herself, and allowed Nelson to tug her up the
remaining steps. Then they did a lap around the church.
From the outside St Mary's was a typical twelfth century
building – solid and squat and not in the least decorative. Liz
had almost reached the point in the graveyard where they'd
started, when a huge, shaggy shape detached itself from
behind one of the toppling gravestones.

Nelson gave a 'yip' of delight and greeted Skipper's
wolfhound Griff. As Liz looked, Skipper's towering figure
came around the side of the church, dressed in yellow
oilskins. As he got closer, Liz saw he was hatless, and there
were water drops on his eyelashes and in his beard.

'Hello!' Liz greeted him warmly. 'I wasn't expecting to see
you this morning. I thought you'd be out on the *Stella*.'

'I gave the lads a few days off. Potsy's been moaning
about needing a holiday, even though we all had a break in
March.'

There was a beat of awkward silence. Skipper's usually
open expression was grim, closed off. Liz guessed it wasn't
the rain.

'Are you okay?' she asked.

He looked down at her with his shrewd blue eyes. 'Not

really. If Christian'd been safely with me on the *Stella* he'd still be alive.'

That was probably true.

He saw her expression and gave a wry smile. 'This is where you're supposed to say "Oh no, it's not your fault."'

'It's not your fault. No, really, it's not. You had no choice but to lay Christian off. Under the circumstances.'

'Juliette knows nothing about that. She won't see me.'

'Give her time. She's still very raw.'

They fell silent as Nelson chased Griff around the grave-stones. Nelson had no real chance of catching the bigger dog, but Griff had adopted a half-hearted lope that made him think he might. It was quite sweet to watch.

Skipper spoke again. 'I bumped into Mike Howson on my way up here. He told me what happened at the gallery last night.'

'Ah.' She thought about telling Skipper she'd been there, but decided not to. She already had a reputation in the town for always being in the thick of trouble.

Skipper continued. 'He told me the gallery discovered one of their paintings was fake too.' He wiped the rain out of his eyes. 'Poor Dennis.'

'Dennis?'

'I should think the police will want to talk to him about it.' He saw her blank expression. 'You don't know Dennis? I thought everyone did.'

Liz shook her head. 'Why would the police want to talk to him?'

'Dennis Kitson? You really haven't heard of him?'

Liz shook her head again.

Skipper gave a disbelieving smile. 'He's probably the

UK's most famous art forger. And he lives right here in Whitby.'

WHEN SHE GOT BACK HOME, Liz dried herself and Nelson off, and went up to the sitting room to switch on her laptop. As she waited for the ancient machine to grind into life, she inspected her sitting room walls. Niall had done a good job of cleaning the soot off the woodwork and floor, but the walls were more porous and still had grubby streaks on them. She would have to repaint – another expense she hadn't budgeted for. Her screen flickered on, and she sat down, glad of the distraction from her finances.

She typed DENNIS KITSON into the search bar, expecting to have to trawl through the results to find what she was looking for. Instead, the match was immediate. He had his own Wikipedia page.

> **Dennis Kitson** (born 1962) is a British artist and former art forger. Over an eighteen-year period, between 1989 and 2007, he produced a large number of forgeries that he successfully sold internationally to museums, auction houses, and private buyers, accruing nearly £1 million.
>
> He is most famous, however, for his involvement in the **Knightsbridge Museum heist**, carried out in 2005 but not discovered until 2007, thanks to his skilful forgery of Ruben's famous **Rape of the Sabines**.

There were other articles too, mainly about Kitson's trial and sentencing. After his arrest he got four years for the museum robbery, plus another two for other misdemeanors taken into account. He'd ended up serving five years in total, and was released in 2013.

The images she found were mostly photos from his trial. She could see it wasn't only his proficiency with a paintbrush that had attracted attention from the media. He had a square jaw and long blond hair, much like a rock star, or a football player. The flamboyance of his crime, combined with his looks, had made him something of a hero in anti-establishment circles.

Several pages through the search she found something even more interesting.

FIND DRAWING CLASSES NEAR YOU. Need a Drawing Class? *We've found the top* Drawing Classes *near you.*

The first on the list for Whitby was the Brunswick Life Drawing Class. The tutor was Dennis Kitson. And there was a mobile phone number.

Her call was answered by the man himself.

'Hello. I'm not here. Please leave your number after the beep. Beeeeep.' He chortled. 'Only kidding.'

'Mr Kitson?'

'For my sins. How can I help you?'

'I just got your number online. For your life drawing classes. I'd love to come along to one.'

'Ah, that's a pity. I'm fully booked for this block. Call me in August. I might have some places next term.'

'Oh'.

He must have heard the disappointment in her voice. 'I'm sorry.'

Liz thought fast. 'Is it possible I could just come along as a spectator? To see what you do?'

'I don't see why not. Although it looks like I'm going to have to cancel the class tonight anyway. My usual–' He broke off. There was a thoughtful pause on the other end of the line.

'Mr Kitson?'

'Still here, love. You say you're keen to see what we do?'

'I am.'

'Exactly *how* keen are you?'

They met at seven o'clock outside the Brunswick Centre on Brunswick Street. The massive building had originally been a church, but was now available to rent for local events. At first she didn't recognise Dennis Kitson from his online photos. His dirty blond hair was now streaked with grey and tied up in a ponytail. His face was heavily lined, but his blue eyes still held a glint of mischief as he unlocked the door. The air inside the church was chilly, much chillier than it should have been in early June. Liz shivered as she gazed around the large, shadowy space that was circled by a wooden balcony. Dennis showed her into the vestry, a little room to one side of the organ. It smelled of dust and damp.

'You can leave your things in here. They should be okay.' He pointed to a floral dressing gown that was hanging on a hook on the wall. 'Put that on when you're done. I'll go and get everything set up, and come and get you when we're ready.' He grinned at her. 'You're a sport, Mrs McLuckie, I'll give you that.'

When he'd gone, Liz sat down on the bench. Was she completely mad? What had seemed like a good idea that morning now just felt bizarre. What on earth was she thinking? As she sat, she heard other voices echo with Dennis's in the church hall. She had two choices. Get up and leave, or...

she slowly started to undress. At her age – and an ex-nurse to boot – she should be beyond embarrassment. The sound of voices got louder. How many people were out there? She pushed the thought away and thought instead about Christian Petit. He had died during the burglary at the West Cliff Gallery, and she was convinced that the burglary had something to do with the fake *Rockpool* painting. It was too much of a coincidence for it not to be. It was also too much of a coincidence that a world-class fake had been discovered in the same town as a world-class faker. She was doing this for Juliette and Christian. Also, if she was honest, for her own curiosity.

As strong as her curiosity was, she still hesitated before unhooking her bra. Really? Was she really doing this? She decided she was. She took off her bra and her pants, ignoring the draught that sent goosebumps over her skin and stiffened her nipples. She quickly tugged the dressing gown on. It smelled of stale perfume and turpentine.

She sat down again and wondered what to do about her feet. She really didn't want to go barefoot across the splintery floor of the church hall. She took her socks off and pushed her feet back into her trainers. She could take them off at the last minute.

There was a knock at the door, that made her jump. Dennis opened the door and stuck his head in. 'All good? We're ready for you.'

Liz followed him out into the church hall, feeling like she was going to her own execution. She lifted her chin and told herself she was a strong, modern woman, who wasn't ashamed of her body. There was a low podium in the centre of the hall, made from two wooden pallets, circled by easels. From her quick glance at the students she saw they were all older women... except... Liz's heart fell through her boots as she saw a face she knew. Skipper was as surprised to see her as she was to see him – his eyes widened. She saw the beginning of a grin creep over his lips as she tore her eyes away and stepped up onto the podium, where there was a stool waiting. She saw Dennis's encouraging nod, and, face flaming, took off the dressing gown.

'Trainers?' prompted Dennis.

'Oh, yes. Sorry.' She slipped her trainers off and Dennis put them to one side of the podium.

'We'll have your left hand on your left knee, I think. And your body turned slightly to the right. That's it... Lift your chin a bit... Perfect.'

Luckily, it wasn't an elaborate pose, and she was turned away from Skipper... but towards another face she knew. Dora Spackle's eyebrows had disappeared into her hairline with shock. Head curator of the Abbey Museum, Dora had occasionally helped, but more often hindered Liz's previous investigations. She was prickly at best, and usually downright rude. Liz looked at her outraged expression and felt a surge of anger. If Dora wanted to take life drawing classes, then *someone* had to pose naked. If not her, then somebody else. Dora's lips pursed. Liz had to swallow the burst of slightly hysterical laughter that rose in her throat.

'Okay, people,' Dennis addressed his circle of students. 'Tonight you only have one hour. Bearing that in mind, keep it loose, look at the overall shape, and don't overwork the detail.'

As the artists bent to their paper, or lifted their thumbs to measure some part of Liz's anatomy (she didn't care to imagine which) she locked her eyes on a spot above Dora's head and stayed very, very still. She was careful never to meet Dora's eyes, or to glance to her left, in Skipper's direction.

It was the longest hour of her life.

She thought she might faint with relief when Dennis eventually clapped his hands.

'That's all, folks,' he said. 'Step away from your easels and let's have a look.' He turned to her. 'Thanks, love. You can get dressed now.'

Liz grabbed the dressing gown to make herself decent, retrieved her trainers and made a dash for the vestry, stiff from having sat in one position for so long.

After she dressed, she sat in the vestry until everything had gone quiet outside. She *really* didn't want to see Dora or Skipper. When she finally judged it was safe, she crept back into the hall, where she found Dennis folding up the easels.

'Thank you, Mrs McLuckie. You're a trooper. I think I might be able to squeeze you into my class next week, under the circumstances.'

'Thank you.' Liz hadn't had the chance to ask him any questions during the class. She knew no more about Dennis Kitson than she had before her ordeal, but she really didn't have the energy to ask him anything now. 'I'll see you next week.'

Skipper was waiting for her outside. She felt her face flame as she saw him.

'I don't know about you,' he said, his blue eyes crinkling with humour, 'but I really need a drink.'

They went to the White Horse and Griffin. After they bought their drinks, they found a vacant table near the door. The public bar of the White Horse was very long, narrow and dark. Skipper looked huge and vivid in the confined space.

'Well done,' he said as they sat down.

She gave him a sceptical look.

'No, really. I thought you did very well. And so did I. I think that's the best drawing I've ever done.' He took a gulp of his beer. 'I might even frame it.'

Her eyes flashed to his in alarm, and she saw he was teasing. They both laughed. Skipper raised his pint in a toast.

'To art,' he said.

'To art.' They clinked glasses.

A thought occurred to Liz. 'I'd better call Niall and let him know I'll be late.'

She searched her bag in vain. 'Oh no!' She turned to Skipper with a crestfallen expression. 'I must have left my phone at the centre. I'm always losing it. Do you think Dennis will still be there?'

'If we hurry.' Skipper saw her questioning look. 'I'll come with you.' He took another quick gulp of his beer before they left. To his credit, he left his almost untouched pint on the table without a backward glance.

When they got back to the Brunswick Centre they tried the door. It was still open.

'We're in luck,' said Skipper. 'He's still here.'

They pushed their way in. Although the lights in the hall were off, it wasn't completely dark, because there was still some daylight outside and the streetlights had just come on, shining through the tall leaded windows. There was no sign of Dennis.

'I probably left it where I got changed,' said Liz, her voice echoing in the empty space. Skipper accompanied her across the hall and waited for her outside the vestry as she went in. She found her phone on the bench. They headed back through the hall together.

'Do you think he just forgot to lock up?' said Liz.

'I'll call him and let him know.' Skipper took his phone from his pocket and dialled. After a moment, Liz heard a sound, somewhere nearby. It took her a few moments to recognise the *Rocky* theme tune, or an approximation of it. Skipper heard it too, and hung up.

'Dennis!' he called. 'Dennis!'

No answer.

'He must have left his phone here too,' suggested Liz.

'And forgot to lock the door?'

Liz shrugged. 'These things happen. Call him again. We can follow the sound.'

Skipper did as she suggested, and the *Rocky* theme tune led them across the hall and through the door to the right of the organ, where the public toilets were.

'Dennis?' Skipper put his ear to the door of the men's room. 'In here.' He tried the door, and it was unlocked. He went in.

He came out again almost immediately, his face ashen.

'We have to call the police,' he said.

It took a moment for his words to sink in. 'He's not...?'

Skipper nodded.

'A heart attack? Or...?' She hesitated, tempted to go in and see for herself.

'You don't have to look. Just take my word for it. He's very, very dead.' He pulled his mobile phone from his pocket. She stopped him with her hand on his arm.

'What?' he asked, with a frown.

'I can't be here. I really can't... Flint.'

Understanding dawned on his face.

She stared up at him. 'What am I going to do?'

L iz ran the roller over the wall and stared at it. The paint was covering the soot smears nicely, but she wasn't sure she was happy. She hadn't been able to get the same shade of off-white at the hardware store, and the new paint was a little whiter than the original. It looked a bit too stark against the beams and worn flagstones. Liz stood back and squinted at the section of wall she had almost finished. Perhaps she'd be able to get the original paint online? She probably never should have started with the whiter paint, but had decided to go ahead anyway and cover up the soot smears, to distract herself from thoughts of Dennis Kitson.

Poor Dennis. She still had no idea whether he'd died of natural causes, or... She didn't want to think about the alternative. She looked again at the wall. Should she stop painting, or keep going?

She was interrupted by a knock at the door. She peered out of the window and could just see the top of Kevin's head.

'Come in!' she shouted. 'I'm upstairs.'

She heard Kevin let himself in, and Nelson's 'yip' of greeting.

'I'll be down in a mo!' she called. She put the roller back in the tray and wiped her hands on a paper towel. She wasn't a tidy decorator. No matter how hard she tried she always managed to get more paint on herself than on whatever she was painting. She heard Kevin running water in the kitchen.

'I hope you don't mind,' he said when she joined him. He'd filled the kettle and put it on the stove. 'I'm dying for a cuppa.'

'Of course not. *Mea casa sua casa.* Do you want biscuits? There's some in the tin.'

'Great!' Kevin found the biscuit tin and took a handful of digestives. He sat at the table. 'I'm starving. I didn't manage to get breakfast this morning. Flint wanted us all in early doors.'

Liz thought about asking him why, and decided not to. She had to be careful.

'I could make you something, if you like? Eggs? Bacon?'

'No, you're alright. I don't have long.' He bit into a digestive and spoke around it, scattering crumbs. 'We had another DB last night. A guy called Dennis Kitson. Do you know him?'

Liz shook her head, but was careful not to meet Kevin's eyes. She busied herself putting teabags into the mugs instead.

'Natural causes, was it?' She had to ask. She simply couldn't help herself.

'Very much *not* natural. He'd been strangled.'

'Oh. Do you think it has anything to do with Christian Petit?'

'We're not sure yet. There is a connection, but it's tenuous. We're following leads.'

'I see.'

'You've been busy.'

'Sorry?' Her heart thumped in alarm.

He nodded at her overalls. 'Painting again?'

She laughed, but even to her ears it sounded forced. 'Yes. There was a bird in the sitting room. Soot on the walls.'

She was glad when the kettle boiled and she was able to bustle about getting milk, etc, but eventually she had to join Kevin at the table. She gave him his mug.

'Have you proposed to Anna yet?' She thought a change of subject was a good idea.

Kevin pulled a face. 'I haven't found the right moment. We're going away for the night on Friday. I'll do it then.'

'Good luck.'

'Thanks.'

'I'll see you before that, though, won't I? It's Mahjong night tonight.'

'Sorry. I'm going to have to cancel our session. Overtime.'

'That's a pity.' She managed to make more inconsequential conversation while Kevin drank his tea. Eventually he drained his mug.

'Better dash.' He was about to get to his feet, when he paused. 'I forgot. I have something for you.'

He took a sheet of folded paper from his jacket pocket and gave it to her.

'What is it?' she asked. But she guessed what it was before she'd unfolded it completely: a charcoal sketch of a naked woman.

'We found quite a few of these in the Brunswick Centre. Some are better than others, but...'

Liz blushed. She couldn't think of a single thing to say.

'So?' prompted Kevin. 'Is there anything you want to tell me?'

'I was with Skipper when he found Dennis. I thought... under the circumstances... I shouldn't bring that to Flint's attention.'

'Probably a good idea.'

'She hasn't seen the sketches, has she?'

'No. I managed to round them up before she got there. I take it it's not a coincidence, you turning up at Dennis's class?'

'I heard he was an art forger. A good one. After the painting at the gallery turning out to be fake...'

'As usual we were a step behind you. But only a step. You have to be careful, Liz, or you'll get trodden on. Heavily.'

'I know. I'm sorry.'

'Why didn't you tell me? You know I have your back, don't you?'

'I didn't want to put you in an awkward situation. Again.'

Kevin gave a hollow laugh. 'Believe me, I'm used to it by now. Please be honest with me in future, eh?'

Liz nodded.

He wasn't going to let her off that easily. 'Promise?'

'Promise.'

'Good.' He got to his feet. 'Just for the record, I'd have guessed you were involved even without the sketch.'

'How?'

'When I told you about Dennis, you asked me hardly anything about him. That's not the Liz I know.'

When Kevin had gone, Liz continued with her painting. Even though the colour wasn't right she decided she didn't have the time or the mental bandwidth to sort it out. It would have to do for now.

As she painted, she thought about the conversation she'd had with Kevin. She knew he wouldn't tell Flint she'd been with Skipper when he discovered Dennis's body, and hoped that Flint would never find out. She'd hate to get Skipper into trouble. She'd been so relieved when he suggested she should just make herself scarce from the Brunswick Centre. Not many people would have done that. He was a good man. And attractive. She hadn't realised that at first, when she'd first seen him give his eulogy at Daniel Holliday's memorial in March, but now she knew him better she found she liked looking at him.

'For God's sake, woman!' Realising the direction her thoughts were taking, Liz steered them back to safer waters. Benedict. She hadn't seen him since she'd left him with Constance on the night of the party, and now that Mahjong was cancelled she wouldn't necessarily see him tonight either. Perhaps she should call him and invite him to dinner?

She realised she had no paint left in the tray. When she went to refill it, she found it was down to the dregs of the paint in the tin. Frustratingly, there was only a narrow section of wall still to do, but there wasn't enough paint to stretch that far. She couldn't leave it, because there would be a demarcation line between the old shade and the new one.

She tidied herself up, then roused Nelson and they set off for the hardware store together. They had reached the end of the cobbled section of Church Street and were about to turn left towards the bridge, when Liz saw a familiar figure pushing a buggy.

'Juliette!' she called. The French woman kept walking. Liz put on a burst of speed, a change of pace that delighted

Nelson. Eventually she caught up with her. 'Juliette. Didn't you hear me?'

Juliette stopped the buggy and turned to glare at Liz.

'What's the matter?' asked Liz, dismayed.

'I saw you. In the gallery. Don't pretend you weren't there.'

'And what did you think I was doing?'

Juliette frowned, unsure what Liz was getting at.

'You asked for my help. I was taking a look around. Hoping I could find out something useful.'

'You said you weren't going to help me.'

'I changed my mind.'

Juliette's eyes filled with tears. She blinked them back. 'Did you find out anything?'

'Not really. Your act of sabotage took centre stage. Did the police charge you?'

'No. They gave me a warning, but didn't arrest me.'

'That's something, at least.' James Bullington wouldn't be happy about that. Liz had to take her hat off to Flint for not letting him bully her. 'In the days before he died, Juliette, did Christian say anything, or do anything out of the ordinary?' She really hadn't known Christian that well, but was aware he'd been in prison in France. It had occurred to her that he might somehow have been complicit in the break-in. An inside job turned sour?

Juliette pulled a face. 'He had been very down. But in that last week he changed. He told me our luck had changed for the better.'

'How?'

'He would not tell me. But he was happier, certainly.'

Liz was thoughtful. That certainly fit with her theory that

Christian might have been involved in the break-in. But why had the burglars killed him?

Juliette was watching her closely. 'I know what you are thinking. But my Christian was a good man. He was unlucky in France. How do you say it? He had "fallen in" with bad people? But since we came here, since Giselle was born, he was heading straight.'

Liz looked deep into Juliette's eyes – Juliette believed what she was saying. But that didn't necessarily make it true.

8

L iz bought another tin of paint at the hardware store, then stopped off at the Full Moon Café. Nelson ran to get his plastic pig as soon as she unclipped him, while she perched herself on a stool at the counter.

'Hello, stranger,' said Tilly with a grin. 'Where've you been?'

'WE KNOW WHAT YOU'VE BEEN DOING,' bellowed Iris, who was sitting at one of the nearby tables. 'DON'T WE, DICKIE?'

Dickie just smiled and nodded. He was watching Iris eat a jam scone. He didn't have a sweet tooth, having spent most of his life as a jockey, watching his weight. Old habits died hard.

'TUT TUT! NAUGHTY GIRL!'

Liz looked at Tilly, and then at Gryzna, Tilly's statuesque Belarussian assistant manager. They both smirked at her.

'What on earth are you talking about?' she asked.

Gryzna grabbed a teatowel and held it provocatively in front of herself. 'Da da dah dah,' she sang.

'DA DA DAH DAH,' added Iris gleefully.

Liz realised they were singing the striptease music. Gryzna whipped the teatowel away with a flourish.

'Who told you?' asked Liz wearily. She hoped it wasn't Skipper. She'd thought he was more discreet than that.

'Dora. She made a point of coming in this morning just to spread the news. To us, and anyone else who would listen.'

Tilly grinned. 'I never had you down as an exhibitionist, Liz.'

'I DID!' exclaimed Iris. 'SHE'S A WOMAN OF MANY PARTS. AREN'T YOU?'

Gryzna laughed when she saw Liz's crestfallen expression. 'I would not worry about it. It is news today, but everyone will have forgotten about it tomorrow.'

'I certainly hope so.' And in the meantime, she hoped it wouldn't reach the ears of Detective Inspector Flint.

'TERRIBLE ABOUT POOR OLD DENNIS KITSON, THOUGH, EH?' Iris's face grew serious. 'WHAT A WAY TO GO. THROTTLED IN A TOILET.'

'Terrible,' agreed Liz. She took the mug of tea Tilly passed to her. 'That's common knowledge, then?'

Tilly nodded. 'You know what this town's like. Everyone's saying his past eventually caught up with him.'

'PITY HIS POOR DAUGHTER,' sniffed Iris.

'His daughter?' prompted Liz.

'SHE LIVES UP ON BOULBY BANK. DENNIS LIVED WITH HER. SHE'LL BE SHOCKED, BUT SHE SHOULDN'T BE – YOU LIVE BY THE SWORD, YOU DIE BY THE SWORD, EH, DICKIE?'

Dickie nodded.

That was a possibility, Liz supposed. Maybe Dennis's death had nothing to do with the gallery break-in? Maybe it was some of his criminal connections catching up with him? All the same, given the fake painting in the gallery, it was a hell of a coincidence.

'What can I get you to eat?' asked Tilly. 'Mags has just made some flapjacks.'

'Sounds good. I'll take two, and a couple of prawn rolls to go, please.'

She took Nelson and the paint home, then retraced her steps to Grape Lane with the goodies from the café and a flask of tea. Benedict was surprised to see her.

'I thought I'd bring you some lunch,' said Liz.

He looked at his watch. 'I didn't realise it was that time already. Shall we eat outside? Give me five minutes and I'll be with you.'

Liz headed out to the back of the museum, where there was a little garden that overlooked the harbour, and a bench that the sun had just reached. She unpacked the sandwiches and waited. Benedict was longer than the five minutes he had promised, but eventually came out, looking a little harassed.

'Sorry, I just needed to be sure Patrick was on top of things.' Patrick was one of the volunteers who worked in the museum.

'Sandwiches first, or flapjack?' asked Liz.

'Savoury before sweet, I think.' He kissed her and took a prawn roll. 'Thank you.'

They ate in silence for a minute or so, before Benedict spoke again.

'Dora Spackle came to see me this morning.'

Liz's heart sank. 'She told you about the art class.'

'She did. She said she knew you and I were an item, and thought I should know what you were up to.'

'Bloody woman.' Liz knew that Dora liked to stir things, but this was a new low, even for her.

'Since when were you posing at art classes?' asked Benedict. 'You've never mentioned it.'

She glanced at him, but his expression was shuttered. She genuinely hadn't thought it would be a problem. It was *her* body, after all.

'It was just spur of the moment. A one-off thing. You don't mind, do you?'

'Of course not. It really has nothing to do with me, does it?'

But there it was: the almost imperceptible flicker of the muscles at the corner of his lips – his tell.

'Are you sure?' she probed. 'You are entitled to an opinion, you know.'

'I'm sure.' But he was careful not to look at her, and quickly changed the subject. 'Kevin's cancelled Mahjong tonight.'

'Yes. I know. We can do something else if you like. Go for a drink?'

'Actually, I have quite a lot of paperwork I need to catch up on. I might just have a night in if that's okay?'

'Of course.' She made a show of pouring them both tea from the flask, thinking it was a very good thing that *she* didn't have a tell to betray her.

After Liz had finished painting her wall she decided she needed some air to clear her head, so she took Nelson out for another walk. They headed over to the West Cliff beach. By that time it was almost five o'clock, so they had the beautiful beach mostly to themselves. They walked along the wet sand near the water's edge, past the line of multi-coloured beach huts. There were only a few huts currently in use, but Liz knew that would change when the school holidays started, when they would be mobbed by sandy families with all their deckchairs and buckets and spades. She and Nelson walked for another few minutes, then turned around and headed back again. All the time, thoughts were churning in Liz's head. Had Benedict been off with her, or was it her imagination? She didn't like to think she'd upset him, but on the other hand she was too old to ask for permission to do the things she wanted. Perhaps she was too set in her ways to be in a relationship, too used to being on her own since Mark's death? Did Benedict object to other people seeing her naked? Why? Because of some macho sense of ownership? Or perhaps he was ashamed of her? Liz didn't like either of those options, and realised she wouldn't know unless she asked.

As they got back to the Pavilion car park she saw a figure with red hair about to get into a small sports car.

'Brian!'

'Mrs McLuckie!' The gallery assistant gave her a lopsided smile. 'How nice to see you. Are you well?'

'Fine, thanks. How are things in the gallery?'

Brian sighed. 'Not great, if I'm honest. People have been staying away in droves. Not surprising, I suppose.'

'Can I ask you a question?'

'If you like.'

'Why did Mr Bullington decide to open a gallery here? Isn't Whitby a bit out off the beaten track for high-end art?'

Brian gave a wry chuckle. 'You're right. It doesn't make a lot of sense, does it? James was born in Robin Hood's Bay and wanted to come back to his roots after leaving London.'

'It's been a struggle, then?'

'You could say that. Last year was a hard one, but it looks as if things are picking up now. Or at least, they *were*, before this break-in business, and poor Mr Petit's death.'

Liz made an attempt to lighten the tone. 'Business will pick up again soon, surely, though? People forget, don't they?'

'I hope so.' He swung himself into his car. 'See you later.'

He zipped past her as she got to the whalebone arch, and gave her a wave. She waved back. She decided she liked Brian. He seemed quite down to earth in spite of his upmarket, arty profession.

Her phone rang. When she fished it out of her pocket she saw it was Kevin.

'Do you have a minute?' he asked. 'I need some advice.'

She met him at Pannet Park, which was quite close to the police station. They sat on a bench together, with Nelson at their feet.

'I thought I'd just... do it... you know? But now it's nearly time, I have no clue what to do. Do you think I should I get down on one knee? Should do it in the hotel room? Or when we're in the restaurant? Perhaps I should I hide the ring somewhere, and let her find it?' Kevin shook his head. 'It's a nightmare!'

Liz put a hand on his arm. 'It's not the theatrics that make it special, Kevin, it's the emotions.'

Mark had proposed to her at a motorway service station somewhere near Birmingham's spaghetti junction. Not the most romantic spot for a proposal, but she remembered it fondly.

'So... what? You think I should keep it low key?'

'That would be my choice. Propose to her in private, to give both of you space and privacy to enjoy the moment. Then go out to celebrate.'

Kevin nodded. 'You're right. That's what I'll do. I'm not sure Flint will even let me have the weekend off, although I booked it weeks ago.'

'She's still keeping you busy, then?' asked Liz. She saw his suddenly guarded expression. 'Has there been a development in the case?'

He gave her a jaundiced look.

'Oh, come on. You know I'm already invested. And aren't two heads better than one?'

Kevin capitulated. 'It looks like Dennis Kitson *did* fake the Norman Cornish painting.'

'Really?'

'We searched his workshop, up on Boulby Bank. He'd told his daughter he'd given up painting altogether, and she was convinced he had, but we found lots of paint up there, and a canvas prepped for painting. According to Connie the fake was a very good one. Only two or three people in the country could have done it. Dennis was one of them. It's too much of a coincidence, isn't it?'

'It is.' Liz nodded, ignoring his reference to Connie. 'Do you think the forgery was connected to the break-in?'

'It has to be, hasn't it? We just can't work out how. Did the thieves just break in to replace the real painting with a copy? Why? Why didn't they just take the Reynolds?' He hesitated. 'And there's another thing bothering me too.'

'What's that?'

'Christian Petit's post mortem has revealed his time of death. He'd been dead an hour at most when his body was discovered. That was at nine am.'

'So?'

'So the alarm system shows us the time it was disabled, the time the thieves broke in. That was two am. Six hours before Christian died.'

9

The little village of Robin Hood's Bay, about six miles south of Whitby, was very popular with tourists. In the height of the summer it was overrun by sightseers packing the steep, narrow streets and alleyways that ran between the picturesque cottages. Liz was lucky enough to find a space in the public car park at the top of the village, beside the Victoria Inn. She hoped it was still early enough to avoid the worst of the crowds.

The village ran almost vertically down to the sea from the car park, built on a fissure between two steep cliffs. At one time the fishing port at Robin Hood's Bay had been bigger than Whitby's, but it was most famous for having been a smuggling village, notorious for illicit trade in contraband tea, rum, brandy, silk and tobacco. The villagers were known for their ability to outwit customs men, and their success was rumoured to be at least partly due to the network of underground passages that linked the houses. In more recent times the village had become known for fossil hunting, and particularly its ammonites, that could be still found in its cliffs.

Liz made her way down the steep stone steps that led down the hill into the village proper. It was a beautiful morning, still quite cool, and she was enjoying herself.

She'd had the good luck to run into Mike Howson that morning, and had mentioned what Brian had told her about James Bullington coming from Robin Hood's Bay. Mike was happy to confirm that was true, and that Bullington's sisters – Angel and Skye – still lived in the village. Their mother had died the year before, in her nineties, leaving debts that Bullington, Angel and Skye had struggled to pay off. Apparently the old lady had owned racehorses in her heyday, and was still overly fond of a flutter. Mike told Liz that the Bullingtons owned Marnar Dale House, somewhere in the village, although he didn't know exactly where.

She'd decided to go and find it. She doubted she would discover anything useful about the gallery break-in or Christian's death, but – if she was honest – she was glad of the excuse to get out of Whitby for a few hours. As much as she loved the town, it could get a little overwhelming. At least half a dozen people she knew had given her knowing grins or winks in the street. One woman she'd bumped into from her choir had even asked her if she was going to take up modelling full time. Liz could throttle Dora bloody Spackle. She had considered confronting her but had decided against it. The genie was out of the bottle, and there was no getting it back in.

Quite a few people passed Liz, puffing up the steps as she was going down them. Some of the younger ones with backpacks made light work of the climb, but almost everyone else had to pause on the way up. As they were catching their breath they could enjoy the intriguing glimpses of footpaths running off to the left and right, between cottages displaying hanging baskets and tubs filled with geraniums and ivy. There was so much care lavished on the village – everyone made an effort to make it look pretty, especially at that time of year. Many of the cottages were rentals that stood empty for much of the winter, and then in the springtime they were spruced up and made picture-perfect for the tourist season.

Further down the hill, the steps led onto the road, past a stone wall where the ground fell away in a steep ditch to King's Beck, that Liz could hear tumbling over the stones in the bottom. The shops were a delight – gift shops and cafés, shops selling arts and crafts, antiques and toys, chocolate and ice cream. There was even a tiny wet fish shop with glossy green-tiled frontage, and a delicatessen displaying fruit and veg outside.

Liz knew she was getting closer to the sea because she could hear the waves crashing. She turned the corner and eventually saw it, pounding on the cobbled slipway between the sea walls. As it was high tide, there was no sign of the beach. There had been no sign of Marnar Dale House, either, even though Liz had kept an eye out for it on the way down. Beside the slipway stood the Old Coastguard Station, which was now a coffee shop and visitors' centre. Liz decided to call in and ask directions.

When she came out again, she set off back up the hill with renewed purpose. She turned left, as instructed, at the Smugglers' Inn, down one of the narrower paths. The path led past the Coroner's Room, a medieval style building that housed the Robin Hood's Bay museum, and between two rows of cottages that eventually opened out to a wider space, where the cottages continued only on the left hand side, climbing steeply.

The open ground to the right allowed a stunning view down to the rest of the village. Liz admired it as she climbed the hill. The line of cottages ended at a gate with a sign.

MARNAR DALE HOUSE. STRICTLY PRIVATE. NO NOSY PARKERS.

That most definitely excluded her. She hesitated, wondering what to do next. She didn't want to have come for nothing, but did she have the brass neck to just march through? She didn't have an excuse for her visit.

'Bugger.'

The word, spoken quietly but with feeling, came from somewhere in the long grass to Liz's right. As Liz peered into it, the author of the word got to her feet. She was an elderly woman dressed in patched dungarees, a halo of frizzy white hair escaping a bandana. She was holding an empty jar. 'Little bugger got away,' she said by way of explanation. '*Cetonia aurata*. Rare this far north.'

'I see,' said Liz, even though she didn't. 'Do you need a hand?'

The old woman looked her over critically. 'Four eyes are better than two, I suppose.' She beckoned Liz to where she was standing. 'He's in this patch here somewhere. Careful you don't stand on him.'

They both knelt and peered into the patch of grass.

'What exactly are we looking for?' asked Liz

'A beetle. Iridescent green, about three quarters of an inch long. Flashy little bugger. You'll know him when you see him.'

Liz knelt down to search the stalks of grass, nettles and thistles. Her companion did the same. She was just about to suggest they give up because her knees were starting to protest, when she spotted a flash of green.

'There!' she exclaimed, pushing aside some of the vegetation to expose the beetle. She felt her knuckles prickle as she did it.

'Good work!' After a few tense moments of manoeuvering, the old lady succeeded in capturing the beetle in the glass jar and screwed on the lid. They both got to their feet. Liz rubbed her knuckles.

'Nettle sting, eh?' said the other woman with a grin. 'Come with me, and we'll do something about it.'

Liz followed her through the gate.

'Were you on your way to see us?' the old lady asked.

'Erm... no. I was just admiring the view.' In spite of the pain in her fingers, Liz was actually quite pleased with the way things had turned out. It meant she didn't have to make up an excuse for her visit.

The track was overgrown, thick with hawthorn hedges and gorse. It looked as if it had originally been wide enough for a car, but now it could only allow people walking single file.

'I'm Skye Bullington,' said the woman. 'You are?'

'Liz McLuckie.'

'Lucky by name, lucky by nature. This is my first *cetonia aurata*.' Skye peered into the jar as she marched ahead. 'We'll have to find a mate for you now, won't we?'

The track bent sharply to the left, and Marnar Dale House came into sight. It was much bigger than Liz had expected, built into the side of the hill, with many mullioned windows and crooked chimneys, and covered in ivy. There was a sapling growing out of the side of one of the chimneys.

'Home sweet home,' said Skye. She led Liz into the house through the peeling front door. 'Angel! We have a guest!'

After the sunlight outside it took a while for Liz's eyes to adjust. The entrance hall was large, with an oak staircase leading up at the back, and a stone-flagged floor. Every inch of the space was piled with stuff: chairs, broken mirrors, bicycles, stacks and stacks of books. Liz heard footsteps on the stairs.

'Oh, hello.' Another elderly lady peered down at them, dressed in a pink cardigan, pleated skirt and white socks.

'This is Liz,' said Skye. 'She helped me bag a *cetonia aurata*. She has nettle stings.'

'Oh, that's not nice. Come through to the kitchen and I'll give you something for them.'

They went down a few steps into a long, low room that was equally rammed with stuff. Liz could only tell it was the kitchen by the butler's sink and the ancient Aga stove at one end.

'We don't get many visitors,' said Angel. 'Skye scares them off.'

'I do not.'

Angel smiled at Liz. 'She does.' She rummaged in a draw and took out a small jar that she gave to Liz. 'This should do the trick.'

The jar had no label. Liz unscrewed the lid. The contents were a dark, muddy green but smelled pleasant enough.

'You only need a smidge,' said Angel.

Liz put some on her nettle stings.

'Would you like a cup of tea?'

'For God's sake, woman!' snapped Skye.

'What?' Angel looked indignant.

Skye scowled at Liz. 'You don't want a cup of tea, do you?'

'Actually, that would be quite nice.' Ordinarily, of course, Liz would never have dreamed of imposing herself, but she was there on a mission.

'See!' Angel threw her sister a look of triumph, then smiled at Liz. 'I'm afraid my sister has forgotten how to behave with people. I think we have some biscuits too. As long as she hasn't eaten them all.'

'That's what they're there for, aren't they?' huffed Skye. 'If you two are going to cosy up, I'm going to settle this one into his new digs.' She took her jar and its inhabitant out of the room.

As Angel bustled here and there, putting the kettle on the Aga and finding cups, Liz took the opportunity to take a proper look around. There was a lot to see. As well as the books and magazines piled everywhere – on the floor, on the table, on the chairs, on the windowsills – there were a dozen or so illuminated fish tanks on the counters, filled with foliage rather than water. More beetles? Snakes? Spiders? Liz didn't want to think too hard about what might be in them. She distracted herself by looking at the paintings that dotted the walls. They looked original, rather than prints. Some were watercolours, some oils, all landscapes.

'How do you like it?' asked Angel, ladling loose tea into a teapot.

'Not too strong, thanks.'

'Milk?'

'Yes, please.' Liz saw her take a carton of milk out of a bucket of cold water on the floor. Clearly, they didn't have a fridge. When the kettle had boiled, Angel put everything on a tray and carried it to the table.

'Just put those books on the floor. They won't come to any harm. It's a dreadful mess in here. I keep telling Skye this big house is too much for us, and that we should move somewhere we'll be looked after.'

'The Anchorage in Whitby is lovely,' said Liz. 'I have friends there.' She watched Angel set out the cups. 'I see you like art,' she said conversationally, nodding at the pictures on the walls.

'Oh yes. Skye and I are both art lovers. Our brother is too. He owns a gallery.'

'Really?' said Liz, disingenuous. 'Where?'

'Whitby.'

'Not the one that got broken into, I hope?'

Angel blinked. 'Actually, yes. Yes, it was.'

'I'm sorry to hear that. That must have been very upsetting.'

Skye strode back into the kitchen, making Angel jump. 'I hope you're not gossiping, woman. You know I hate gossip.'

'She was just telling me about your brother,' said Liz, coming to Angel's rescue.

'That arsehole,' sniffed Skye.

Liz pressed on. 'I heard there was a do at the gallery last week. Did you go to it?'

'James didn't want us there,' said Angel.

Skye glared at her. 'We would have gone, welcome or not, but we don't have a car.'

'We had to give it up, you know. When mother died.'

'Might as well pile up tenners in the garden and set fire to them,' sniffed Skye.

'Cars *are* expensive to run,' agreed Liz.

'Do you have one, Mrs McLuckie?' asked Angel.

'Yes, I have a Honda.'

'Do you hear that, Skye? Liz has a Honda.'

'I'm very pleased for them both. Have you seen the dustpan and brush?'

'I put them in the bathroom cupboard.'

'Why would you put them in there, for heaven's sake?'

'Because they're red.'

Skye tossed her sister a despairing look and stomped out.

'She knows I keep all our red things together,' said Angel. 'Much neater that way.'

Liz realised she had to make the most of Skye's absence. She took her cup of tea to look at the pictures on the walls.

'These are nice,' she said.

'Aren't they?' Angel joined her. 'None of them are worth very much, I'm afraid. Not like the Cornish.'

'The Cornish?'

'The Norman Cornish. The miner artist? He was a friend of my mother. He painted us playing in a rockpool and gave it to her as a present.' Angel hesitated. 'We don't have it now.'

Liz remembered the figures of the two children on the shore of the painting in the gallery. Angel and Skye? She was surprised they were going to let their brother sell the painting, but perhaps they had no choice. Perhaps they needed the money. As Liz wondered how to turn the conversation back to the gallery, she made a show of looking at the other pictures. One caught her eye. A very simple seascape, with a flamboyant signature: Dennis.

'Dennis,' she said. 'Is that Dennis Kitson?'

'It is. Did you know him?'

'Not very well.'

'We couldn't believe it when we heard the news.' Angel took a tissue from her cardigan pocket and dabbed at her eyes. 'It was awful. Awful.'

'What are you bawling about now?' Skye had come back into the kitchen without Liz noticing. 'She's always moaning about something or other. Carries on something sinful.'

'I'm just sensitive.'

'Crybaby more like.'

'At least I don't have a heart of stone.' Angel glared at her sister.

Liz realised she wasn't likely to find out anything more from Angel, now that Skye had reappeared. She drained her cup. 'My stings feel so much better now.' They did. She couldn't feel them at all. 'I'd better be on my way. Thank you so much for the tea.'

10

A nna turned him down.'

'What?' Liz frowned at Benedict. They were snuggled up together in his conservatory, a beautiful sunny space filled with plants and sleeping cats. 'Did she give him a reason?'

'Several, apparently,' said Benedict. 'She said they were still getting to know each other. That she doesn't believe in marriage. She also thought it was wrong of him to buy a ring before he had her answer.'

'What did Kevin say to that?'

'He broke it off.'

'He *what?*'

'He broke up with her. They came home.'

Liz was silent for a while, letting that sink in.

'Bit of shocker, eh?' Benedict shook his head. 'I didn't see that coming.'

Liz sort of had. Or at least she had anticipated Anna's refusal. But she was still surprised by Kevin's reaction to it.

'Why would he break up with her?' she said. 'I don't understand that "all or nothing" way of thinking.'

Benedict stroked Delilah, who was purring beside him. 'If the relationship is going nowhere it's better to know and finish it, don't you think? Rather than investing more time and energy?'

'You make a relationship sound like a business transaction. Why does it have to *go* somewhere? Why can't it just *be*?'

Benedict seemed puzzled by her questions. 'It's only a natural progression, surely. You're friends, then lovers, then... marriage makes sense. Doesn't it?'

'Is that where you think we're going?' The question was out before Liz had thought about it properly. She pushed away from him so she could see his face properly.

'Well... it's a bit early to tell, isn't it?'

'We're not. I wouldn't marry you.' Liz realised how harsh her words sounded, but felt they were necessary. 'I've been there before, and I'm not going there again.'

'Never? In any circumstances?'

'No.'

Benedict stared at her. Genuinely shocked.

'Sorry,' she muttered. 'I don't know how we got into this conversation.'

Benedict stood up with Delilah, and turned to re-settle the cat on the chair. Liz couldn't see his face. 'Perhaps it's a good thing we did.'

'You're not going to break up with me, are you?' she asked.

'No. Of course not.' Benedict turned back to face her, his expression carefully neutral. 'We don't need to make that kind of commitment, do we?'

But there it was: his tell, tugging at the corner of his lips. Liz couldn't bear it. She stood up.

'I have to get back. I've left Nelson on his own too long.'

Benedict didn't argue. He went with her into the hall.

She hesitated at the door. 'Do you think I should phone Kevin?'

Benedict shook his head. 'I think we should let him lick his wounds in peace for now.'

Liz headed home in something of a daze, oblivious to the sunshine and the scenery. She felt terrible for Kevin, even if it was partly his fault his world had exploded in such a spectacular fashion. She could only think that he really hadn't seen the refusal coming, and had had a visceral, knee-jerk reaction to it. She was betting he was regretting it now.

Just as she was regretting the conversation she'd had with Benedict. Why hadn't she kept her big mouth shut? It was true that she had no intention of marrying him. She had no idea that was the way his thoughts were headed – it was very early in their relationship, after all. She would never have raised the subject if she hadn't been ambushed by it. But it was out there now. There was no taking it back.

She heard a tapping sound, and looked around. To her surprise she saw she was on Sandgate, outside the café. She didn't even remember crossing the bridge. The tapping was Tilly, knocking on the café window to get her attention. She beckoned her inside. Liz went to the door and Tilly let her in. She'd just been locking up for the night.

'Has B told you? About Kevin? I couldn't believe it when he told me.'

Liz nodded.

'What do you think we should do?'

'It's not really up to us to do anything, is it? Except commiserate.'

'He's not picking up his phone.'

'Maybe he just needs to lick his wounds for a bit,' Liz echoed Benedict's words. 'Let's give him some space.'

'I suppose.'

Liz knew that wouldn't sit easily with Tilly. She was Kevin's oldest friend, and doing nothing wasn't really her style.

'Got time for a coffee?'

Liz nodded. Nelson would be perfectly okay for another hour or so, and Niall was due home soon anyway. She'd lied to Benedict to make her escape, thanking the Gods yet again that she didn't have a tell of her own to betray her.

'Are you okay?' asked Tilly. 'You look a bit peaky.'

'I'm fine,' fibbed Liz. 'Just worried for Kevin, I suppose.'

'Come through to the kitchen. Mags is baking.'

Liz followed Tilly through the beaded curtain. Mags was up to her elbows in dough on the stainless steel workbench. She looked up with a worried expression.

'Liz knows,' said Tilly. 'Benedict told her.'

'Poor Kevin.' Mags gave her dough an emphatic thump. 'He must be devastated.'

'He'd be a lot less devastated if he hadn't been so stupid,' said Tilly.

'For proposing?' asked Liz.

'Of course not. Marriage is a great institution.' Tilly blew Mags – her wife – a kiss. 'But he shouldn't have gone off the deep end when she said no.' She picked up a jar. 'Is instant okay?' she asked Liz. 'I've just switched the machine off.'

'I prefer tea anyway.'

Tilly filled the kettle and clattered it onto the industrial range. 'So what else is new in Liz Land? We haven't seen you for a while.'

'I've been looking into Christian Petit's death. Or trying to, at least.'

'And?' Tilly's eyes lit with curiosity.

'And I haven't got very far.'

'Flint's been here. Sniffing around. Asking where I was on the night of the break-in. I told her that kind of job wasn't really my style. If I were her, I'd have someone else in my sights. *Two* someones, actually. They've both done time for similar jobs.'

'Did you tell Flint that?'

'Of course not. But they're bound to be on her radar.'

'Who are they, and where would I find them?'

Tilly grinned. 'Do you really want a cup of tea? Or do you fancy something stronger?'

THE ANGEL HOTEL on New Quay Road was once Whitby's principal coaching inn, running coaches to York, Scarborough and Sunderland. Although its appearance had altered quite a lot since the nineteenth century – it now had a glass-fronted extension with a roof terrace – it hadn't changed in spirit. The 'pub with rooms' was very popular with visiting stag parties and locals looking for fun on a night out. As it was Friday evening, the tables outside were already filled with laughing and chattering drinkers. It was a bit quieter inside, and there were still a few tables free.

'What do you fancy?' asked Tilly.

'G and T, please.'

While Tilly got the drinks, Liz found a free table. When Tilly came back she didn't sit down.

'Don't get comfortable there,' she said. 'There's someone I want you to meet.' She nodded towards a figure in a corner of the bar – a man sitting on his own, dressed in double denim. As they got closer Liz saw he had thinning hair and the high colour of a drinker.

'Keith!' Tilly slapped him on the shoulder. 'How's things?'

'Mathilda.' The man gave a start of surprise. 'Haven't seen you for a while.'

'Oh, you know how it is. Busy, busy. How about you? Still at Skinningrove?'

'Nah. I jacked that in.' He rubbed one of his reddened cheeks. 'Let's just say I'm considering my options.' His watery eyes found Liz.

'This is my friend Liz,' said Tilly. 'Liz, this is Keith Braithwaite.' She nodded at his glass that only had half an inch of beer in it. 'Can I get you a drink?'

Braithwaite brightened. 'Don't mind if you do. I'll take a pint of Hook.' He hesitated, then decided to go for it. 'And a Grouse chaser.'

Tilly shot him a jaundiced look – they both knew he was chancing it – but headed to the bar anyway.

Liz and Braithwaite gazed at each other, awkward.

'So... Elaine,' he began.

'Liz.'

'Liz. What do you do?'

'I have a couple of Airbnbs, on Henrietta Street.'

'Nice. Don't suppose you're looking for a handyman? I'm pretty good with a screwdriver.'

'Not really. No. Sorry.'

He shrugged. 'Shy bairns get nowt. I thought I would ask.' As he ran his hand through his hair, Liz saw it was trembling slightly. She dredged her brain for something to say.

'How do you know Tilly?'

He snorted, then peered at Liz, as if assessing what she might know. Eventually he decided to play it safe. 'Oh, you know, I see her around.'

'You're not from Whitby?' Liz thought she'd detected a slight Geordie accent.

'Sunderland.'

Not Geordie, then, but close. 'I had an aunt in Seaham.'

'Aye?'

Their conversation continued awkwardly. Liz was relieved when Tilly rejoined them, carrying Braithwaite's beer and whisky.

'There you go,' she said as she put it on the bar beside him.

'Thanks, Mathilda. You're a gent.'

'We'll leave you to it, Keith. Take care, eh?'

'Will do.' He took no notice of them as they moved away, concentrating instead on taking an impressive slug of his beer.

Liz and Tilly found a free table near the window and sat down.

'Poor bugger,' said Tilly. 'He's always liked a drink, but I hadn't realised he'd been hitting the bottle so hard. It would take a steady nerve to disable an alarm as sophisticated as the one at the gallery.'

'Not to mention the CCTV. You think we can rule Braithwaite out?'

'I think so.'

Liz stirred the ice in her gin and tonic. 'What about the other guy you mentioned? The other "likely lad".'

Tilly sipped her wine and looked thoughtful. 'It's Saturday tomorrow. Do you have anything planned?'

'COME ON, YOU SEASIDERS!'

Liz winced as the man in the seat behind her bellowed into her ear, almost deafening her. She wondered – not for the first time – what on earth she was doing there. It was raining – a real Yorkshire downpour. Even though they were sitting in the covered stand of the Turnbull Ground, they were right at the front and weren't really protected. Her cagoule was keeping the worst of it off, but her trousers and shoes were soaked.

The players were faring no better. Both sides – Whitby Town and Belper Town – were slipping and sliding on the wet grass and churned-up mud in front of the goals. So far it was a nil-nil draw.

'Here you go.' Niall pushed his way through to them with three cups of coffee from the mobile van. 'Sorry, Liz, they didn't have decaf.'

The coffee wasn't great but Liz clutched it anyway for the warmth. Tilly nudged her, almost knocking the cup out of her hands.

'There! That's Snaky.' She pointed to one of the referee's assistants on the far side of the pitch, a tall, thin man with a goatee beard. 'Snaky Stevenson. I thought he'd be here.'

'Couldn't we just have bumped into him somewhere else?'

'I didn't know it was going to be raining, did I?'

'How are we even going to talk to him?'

Tilly pulled a face. 'I don't know. I hadn't really thought about that.'

Liz couldn't hide her relief when the referee blew the half-time whistle.

'That's it,' she said. 'I've had enough. I'm going home.'

'Really?' said Tilly.

'Really. I'm soaked through. We can think of another way to talk to Stevenson. You coming?'

Tilly nodded.

'I might hang on here and watch the second half,' said Niall. He was an avid football fan. Even though Liz and Tilly had stood up, they had to wait, because most of the spectators were heading out to find better shelter or half-time sustenance. Finally, the crowd started to move. Liz and Tilly were about to head up the stairs when they were stopped by a shout.

'Fairweather!' It was the man Tilly had pointed out as Snaky Stevenson. He ran to the front of the stand and glared at Tilly, his hair plastered down with rain and his linesman's strip clinging wetly. 'I have a bone to pick with you. You set the bizzies on me.'

Tilly was outraged. 'You calling me a snitch?'

'If the glove fits.'

'I never said anything.'

'So how come Flint came to me and Keith Braithwaite straight after talking to you?'

'Don't you think she might have had you in her sights already? Ex-cons living in the area? It hardly takes Sherlock Holmes to work it out.'

'Don't get smart with me.' Stevenson scowled.

'I never mentioned you to her. Or Keith.'

'Yeah, right.' Stevenson clearly wasn't convinced. 'It's a good job I was playing poker that night and have an alibi, or they would have dragged me into the station.'

'I wouldn't snitch on anyone,' insisted Tilly. 'Even you.'

'Even me?' Stevenson stepped belligerently up to the hoarding that separated them. 'What's that supposed to mean?'

'Whoa there, big fella,' Niall stepped in. 'You really going to square up to a lady?'

'Lady?' sneered Stevenson. 'This one? Don't make me laugh.' He turned on his heel and strode off.

They all stared after him.

'I reckon that's your man,' said Tilly. 'His poker cronies would say anything to back him up.'

But Liz wasn't so sure. 'You know, the thieves may not even be local. In fact, the more I think about it, the more I think they probably aren't. Anybody could see the gallery's website and catalogue, and a provincial gallery is an easy target for a big-time thief.'

Tilly wasn't convinced. 'You think a "big-time thief" is going to walk away from a Reynolds?'

No, she didn't.

Tilly read her look. 'Me neither. So... either the thieves didn't realise how valuable the Reynolds was, or...'

'Or...?' prompted Liz.

'I have no idea.'

11

Liz washed out her emulsion brush under the kitchen tap. In the end she hadn't been able to live with the over-bright shade of white she'd put on the sitting room walls, and so had ordered the original paint online. She'd spent all morning repainting, but was much happier with it now. She should have listened to her inner voice rather than ignoring it.

Nelson whined, and nudged her leg with his nose.

'I'll take you out in a minute. Hold your horses.'

After the excitement of the football match on Saturday she'd spent Sunday with Benedict. They'd had a lovely day, walking on the beach and enjoying a roast lunch at the White Horse and Griffin. Benedict had spent the night, and there had been no mention of the conversation they'd had about marriage. Liz was relieved but suspected he hadn't forgotten it.

She jumped at a knock on the door. Her immediate thought was that it was Kevin. She had texted him a couple of times over the weekend, but had had no reply. When the door didn't open, however, she realised it couldn't be him.

Yip, yip, yip! Nelson barked.

'Coming!' She dried her hands on a kitchen towel and went to open it.

Anna!'

'Hi, Liz.' Kevin's newly ex-girlfriend stood awkwardly on the step. 'I wondered if we could talk?'

'Of course. Come on in.' She ushered her inside. 'Sorry about the mess. I've been painting.'

Nelson greeted Anna, pushing his nose into her hand. She gave him an absent-minded pat. Her face was pale, without make-up, and her hair had been wound carelessly into a knot. Her eyes were puffy, which made Liz think she'd been crying.

'I hope you don't mind me turning up like this. I know how close you and Kevin are.' Anna hesitated. 'How is he?'

'Honestly? I have no idea. He's not replying to my texts.'

'Oh.' Anna looked forlorn.

'Would you like some tea?'

'No, thanks. This is just a flying visit.'

Liz pulled out one of the kitchen chairs so Anna could sit down, and took a seat opposite.

'You've heard what happened on Friday?' asked Anna.

Liz nodded. ''Fraid so.'

'I imagine everyone's blaming me?'

'Actually, no. None of us can believe he reacted so badly.'

Anna sniffed. 'It's not that I don't want to be with him, it's just too early to be thinking about a lifetime commitment, you know?'

'I understand.'

'What do you think I should do?'

'Well, it's hard to say, because I haven't heard his side of the story, but I suggest giving it some time. He'll be disappointed and humiliated. When he's had a couple of days to think it through I'm pretty sure he'll regret breaking up with you. He's probably regretting it already.'

'You think so?'

'I do.' Liz patted her hand. 'What you two have is too good to throw away.'

'I think so too.' Anna stood up. 'I should get back to work before someone misses me.' She forced a smile. 'The dead wait for no one.'

A thought occurred to Liz. 'I don't suppose you did the autopsy on Christian Petit?' She hoped Anna would forgive her clumsy change of subject.

'I did, actually.' Anna didn't seem fazed by it. 'Kevin told me he was a friend of yours?'

'Not exactly. I'm a friend of his wife. But I have a couple of questions.'

'Fire away.'

'How did he die, exactly?'

'He had a large contusion – a blunt-force injury – on the back of his head, and other injuries from impact with the floor. It looked like someone hit him before he fell. He may even have been dead before he went over the bannister.'

'What about his wrists and ankles?'

Anna frowned. 'Sorry, not following you.'

'Did he have any ligature marks?'

'Why would you ask that?'

'He died six hours after the thieves actually broke into the gallery. I was wondering if they might have tied him up.'

'Ah. No. There were no signs of that. Perhaps they locked him up somewhere?'

'Perhaps.'

They both jumped as there was another knock at the door.

Kevin was a couple of steps inside before he spotted Anna. He stared at her, horrified, gave Liz a look of utter betrayal, then spun around and marched out again.

'Kevin!' Liz called after him, but he didn't turn around.

Anna burst into tears.

LIZ WOULD HAVE LIKED to tell Benedict what had happened with Anna and Kevin, but he was at a fundraiser for the Castle Museum in York and was staying overnight there. Niall was doing a shift at the Duke of York, so they ate dinner early. After that, Liz was at a loose end. She tried to read a book in the sitting room, but the smell of the fresh paint started to give her a headache. She put her book down and sighed. She hated it when her friends were at odds with each other, and with her. The look Kevin had given her when he'd seen Anna in her kitchen had cut her to the quick. Was she really expected to take sides?

Liz gazed at Nelson, who was asleep on the hearthrug, his massive head resting on his front paws. If only people were as uncomplicated as dogs! A warm wave of affection washed over her.

'Nelson?'

He opened one eye.

'Fancy another walk?'

He sat up, tongue lolling. Did she really need to ask?

. . .

THEY WENT up the abbey steps, then turned right at the top, taking the footpath that led between the medieval outbuildings of the museum and the Donkey Field. The beach ride donkeys were long gone, thankfully, but the field was still home to a couple of well-fed ponies, and there was a great view of the town from there. Liz stopped for a moment to enjoy it, breathing deeply. The rain at the weekend had cleared the air, leaving it fresh and sweet.

Liz and Nelson continued down the path, past the allotments, to the Ropery. The Ropery was a small ex-council estate that consisted mainly of semi-detached houses and bungalows, and although it was off the beaten track for tourists, it was home to many Whitby residents. Iris had said that Dennis Kitson had lived there with his daughter, but Liz had no idea where. She kept an eye out for any clue as she was walking through the estate, but saw nothing. She headed back to the east quay down Salt Pan Well Steps.

She was about to go past the entrance to Juliette's block of flats, when, on impulse, she decided to pay her a visit. She tied Nelson to a railing at the bottom of the external stairs. He blinked at her accusingly.

'I won't be long, I promise. Be good.'

She headed up the stairs. As she reached the top she could hear some kind of altercation going on inside Juliette's flat. The French woman's voice was raised in anger.

'I do not care how sorry you say you are now! Or what kind of pathetic excuse you have! It was your fault he was there! Yours!'

Liz could see Juliette through the kitchen window, her face pink with fury, but couldn't see the target of Juliette's anger. She could guess, though.

Just as Liz was about to turn away, Juliette spotted her shocked face through the kitchen window. She threw the door open.

'Liz. Come in, please. This... *personne*... was just leaving.'

Even though there wasn't a mark on him, Skipper looked like he'd just gone ten rounds with Mike Tyson. He stared bleakly at Juliette.

'I'm really, really sorry.'

But Juliette wasn't listening. She pointed at the door. Skipper left, with only a fleeting rueful glance at Liz. When he'd gone, Juliette dropped into a chair.

'The nerve of the man.'

Liz didn't know what to say. Her instinct was to put in a few words on Skipper's behalf, but she didn't want to agitate Juliette any further.

'I am sorry you had to hear that, Liz,' said Juliette. 'But it needed saying.'

Liz sat down. 'How are you?'

Juliette shrugged. 'I am waiting for the coroner to release Christian's body. Then I can take him home.'

Home to France. Liz thought it was a real pity Juliette had never felt at home in Whitby.

'I cannot wait to get out of this place,' said Juliette.

'It's actually very nice. You just have to give it a chance.'

Juliette snorted. 'For a nice place, a lot of people seem to die here. Did you hear there has been another one?'

Liz nodded. 'Dennis Kitson. Did you know him?'

'Not personally. Christian used to drink with him sometimes. I was not happy about that. Everyone knew he had been in prison.'

The same as Christian. That was interesting. Why had

Christian promised Juliette things were looking up? Did he suspect – or know – *The Rockpool* was a fake?

Was he blackmailing someone? Dennis? James Bullington?

12

'They're probably here somewhere.' Felicity Kitson swept her arm around the studio. 'Have a good look around, see if you can find them.'

Liz didn't know where to start. She was in Dennis Kitson's studio at the Ropery, which had been converted from a double garage, with two large roof windows that let the sunlight stream in. There were half a dozen or so unfinished landscapes propped on easels, a big trestle table, and stacks of battered Ikea bookcases filled with jars and paints. There was also a paint-spattered Lloyd Loom chair with a paint-spattered cushion. Everything was flecked with paint, including the magazine cuttings and pictures of old masters pinned on the walls.

'What did they look like?' asked Felicity. It was hard to tell how old Dennis's daughter might be. Somewhere in her thirties, perhaps? In contrast to the raddled rockstar looks of her father, she had the smooth skin and wholesome air of a Flemish Madonna.

'Pretty ordinary, really.' Liz had to think fast, inventing

the brushes she said she'd lent to Dennis. 'They were in a blue cloth roll.'

'Odd he should have borrowed them. Dad was really picky about his brushes.'

'Did he do much painting of his own?' Liz changed the subject.

'He gave it up for a couple of years, after... you know.' Felicity continued to rummage on the shelves. 'Everyone thought it was probably for the best. But it made him miserable. He was like a bear with a sore head when he wasn't painting, so I encouraged him to take it up again.' She hesitated. 'I wouldn't have done if I'd known he'd get up to his old tricks. I suppose I should have known better.'

That was more or less what Mike Howson had said to Liz that morning, when he'd given her Felicity's address. 'A leopard can't change its spots.' Liz wasn't sure she totally agreed with him, but in Dennis's case it had certainly seemed to be the case.

She continued searching, raking through the piles of equipment on the floor – old paint rags, bottles of turpentine and distilled water. There was a canvas propped in the corner. The frame seemed old, but the canvas itself looked as if it had been prepped for painting. It had a faded label on the back, with a number and a name – Weston. Liz made a mental note of it, even though she didn't think it would be relevant. She had no idea what she was looking for, if she was honest.

The trestle table looked more promising. It was piled with papers. Liz riffled through them quickly. They were mostly receipts and invoices, including several from Fassbender Dry Art Pigments. There were utility bills too – half a dozen or so brown envelopes, all unopened. Underneath them, Liz found a faded polaroid of Dennis with his arm around a glamorous woman in sunglasses. Liz thought she looked familiar, and looked more closely. The woman was brunette, with a knock-out figure wrapped in a cream bodycon dress. Liz peered at it. She thought the photo had been taken some time in the nineties or early noughties, but still couldn't place the woman's face.

Felicity sighed. 'It doesn't look like they're here, does it? I can't see anything in a blue roll.'

Liz put the polaroids down hastily. 'Perhaps the police took them?'

'It's possible. They did take quite a lot of his stuff. Some of the prints off the walls, and some of the paints. I didn't see any brushes. Maybe you should ask them?'

'That's a good idea.'

'They might not give them to you, even if they do have them.' Felicity frowned. 'Evidence. You know.' For an instant, the woman's capable veneer cracked, and Liz could see the strain underneath. And the grief.

'I'm really very sorry about your dad,' said Liz. 'It was a terrible thing to happen.'

'Yes, well.' Felicity pulled herself together. 'Some people might say he had it coming. You can't play in the dirt without getting dirty, can you?'

'He'd left all that behind, though, hadn't he?'

'I thought so. I really did... But what do I know?'

As they headed for the door, Felicity carefully straightened the cushion on the chair. There was a world of love in the gesture. A world of pain.

'I'm not sure when we'll be able to have the funeral,' she said. 'I hope you'll come.

Dad had a lot of friends, but I haven't seen many of them since he died.'

Liz felt a twinge of guilt for being there under false pretences. Even though she'd only met Dennis briefly, she had liked him.

'He was so...' continued Felicity, groping for words. 'He just loved people. I'd hate for no one to come to his funeral.'

Liz hurried to soothe her. 'Don't worry. That won't happen.' She would make sure of it.

LIZ WALKED HOME up the hill, past the Donkey Field and St Mary's churchyard. On the surface, Felicity seemed to be coping remarkably well with her father's murder, but Liz could imagine how difficult it must be, dealing with the police investigation and all the speculation in the town. Liz felt a little guilty about her ruse. Her exploration of Dennis's studio hadn't yielded any useful clue as to his killer, or how he might be connected to the gallery break-in. She made a mental note to look up Fassbender Dry Art Pigments, but didn't think she would find out anything useful – presumably they were just his paint supplier. Then she remembered the glamorous woman in the polaroid. Liz knew her face. But how? The photo had been taken at least thirty years before.

Rather than going down the abbey steps and having to negotiate a steady stream of holidaymakers and daytrippers, Liz decided to walk down the cobbled lane – Caedmon's Trod – that led down to Church Street beside them. Because most tourists liked to stick to the steps, the lane was empty. She was about a third of the way down when she saw a familiar figure in a cloche hat toiling up the hill towards her

– Dora Spackle, on her way to work at the museum. Liz saw her hesitate, and her realisation that she had no choice but to keep going. She lifted her chin and marched on. Liz had a few moments to decide whether she was going to confront her about her gossiping or not. She decided not to. Why get into a verbal tussle when there could be no winner? She just nodded to Dora and said 'Morning' as she passed.

The look on the other woman's face was priceless. Liz almost laughed out loud. She was still smiling to herself when she put her key in the lock of Gull Cottage a few minutes later. Maybe Dora wouldn't bother spreading gossip about her if she thought she was impervious to it.

Yip, yip. Nelson barked his greeting as she let herself in. He wasn't alone. Niall and Kevin were both sitting at the kitchen table.

'Hello,' she said. 'I wasn't expecting a welcome party. How are you, Kevin?' She was pleased to see him. Perhaps he'd forgiven her for talking to Anna? But, searching his face, she saw his expression was grim. Niall's face was equally joyless. She felt a stab of dread.

'What's going on?' she asked.

'It's Tilly,' said Niall. 'She's been arrested.'

13

'That makes no sense,' said Liz. 'How did Flint even know the equipment was there?'

'An anonymous tip,' said Kevin. 'She used it to get a search warrant for the café.'

'Didn't you have any idea it was going to happen?'

He shook his head. 'Not until Bill Williams told me Tilly was in the cells. Flint kept it quiet. For obvious reasons.'

'The jemmy was definitely used in the break-in?'

'No doubt about it. It still had paint on it from the window of the gallery utility room. It's gone to the labs, but it's pretty clear cut.'

'Whoever broke in must have planted it in the café then tipped Flint off.'

Niall pulled a face. 'There is another explanation.'

Kevin and Liz both stared at him.

'I like Tilly. You know I do. She's a grand woman. But... are we absolutely sure she wasn't involved?'

That was a good question. Tilly had been going straight ever since she and Mags had got out of the Young Offenders

Institution years before. But Liz knew she missed the excitement of her old life.

Liz shook her head. 'There's no way she had anything to do with it. She wouldn't have kept her tools at the café. She'd want to protect Mags.'

'Fair point,' said Niall.

'Guilty or not,' said Kevin, 'she's still screwed.'

They sat in silence, considering that nugget of wisdom.

'Where is Mags?' asked Liz at last. 'Is she at the station?'

Kevin and Niall glanced at each other.

It was Kevin who answered. 'She says she wants nothing to do with it. Or Tilly.'

The last time Mags thought Tilly was up to her old tricks, she threw her out. Liz hoped that wasn't going to happen again.

Kevin stood up. 'I'd better get back to the station and see what's going on. Dad's trying to get her a good solicitor. I hope she's had the sense to say nothing until they get there.'

'I'll go and put some clothes on,' said Niall. Liz realised he was still in a tee shirt and boxer shorts. He disappeared upstairs in a flash of skinny legs.

Kevin headed for the door.

'How are you?' asked Liz.

He just looked at her, his expression stony.

'Anna just turned up here, you know. We weren't sneaking behind your back.'

'It doesn't matter.'

'I think it does. She misses you, Kevin. I think she loves you.'

'Not enough to marry me.' He went out.

.   .   .

WHEN NIALL WAS DRESSED they headed to the police station at Spring Hill. They decided to take Nelson with them rather than leaving him on his own, because they had no idea how long they might be. On the way, they cut down Sandgate and passed the café. It was ten o'clock and the café should have been open, but the lights were off and there was no sign of life.

Whitby police station was a depressing seventies building on the outskirts of town, with absolutely no authority or redeeming features. Liz suffered a twinge of anxiety as she followed Niall inside – she'd spent more hours there than was strictly respectable. The public room was busy, with most of the plastic chairs already taken by people waiting to be seen, including a woman with a toddler in a pushchair. They saw a face they knew.

'Benedict!' Liz hurried to greet him. 'What's happening?'

He kissed her on the cheek. 'I've brought her a solicitor. Seb Galloway. He's in with her now.'

'That's a relief.' Liz felt much better knowing Tilly had representation.

She found a chair beside Benedict, while Niall sat on the floor. Nelson stood between Liz's feet, refusing to sit. He was staring at a man with a snap-back cap, who was sprawled in his chair on the other side of the waiting room. The man scratched his crotch. Nelson growled.

'Hush.' Liz tugged on his lead. 'What's the matter with you?'

Snap-back gave them a thousand-yard stare.

Nelson growled louder.

'You need to take that ugly dog of yours outside,' said snap-back. 'Or I'll come over there and kick it.'

Benedict sat up straighter. 'You'll do no such thing.'

'And who's going to stop me? You?' The man snorted. 'Don't make me laugh.'

Nelson barked. It was very loud in the small space. The baby started to cry. Everyone glared at them.

'It's okay,' said Liz to Benedict. 'I'll take him outside.' But Nelson had decided snap-back was a threat, and no matter how much Liz tugged at his lead or scolded him, he refused to budge.

At that moment the door into the station opened. Flint glared at everyone.

'What is this bloody racket?' She spotted Liz, Niall and Benedict. 'What are you all doing here? This is a police station, not a circus. Go home.'

They had no choice but to do as they were told. When they finally managed to get Nelson outside, Liz saw she had a text. She read it in dismay.

Benedict saw her expression. 'What?'

'It's Mags. She wants us to get Tilly's things from the café.'

'Not good,' said Niall. 'Really not good.'

Mags was waiting for them by the back door to the café. She handed them a hold-all, her face pale but resolute.

'It's just what she needs overnight. She can pick up the rest of her stuff later.'

'Really?' asked Liz. 'Are you sure?'

'I am.' Mags saw Liz's dismay. 'I can't live like this, Liz. Never knowing when she's going to be arrested.'

'She says she didn't do it.'

'So how does she explain the tools?' Mags blinked back tears. 'How could she have kept them *here*, of all places? When we've worked so hard–' She broke off, distressed.

'We think they were planted.'

'By the police?' Mags's eyes widened. 'I know Flint has a vendetta against her but that's...' She couldn't think of a word extreme enough.

Liz shook her head. 'Not the police. Someone else.'

There was an awkward silence. Mags gave them all a level stare. 'I want all of you to look me in the eye and tell me you believe her. One hundred percent.'

Liz held her gaze. She couldn't see what Benedict was doing behind her back, but assumed he was doing the same. Niall wavered. Looked away.

Mags's face hardened. 'Tell her to call me tomorrow.'

When they got home to Gull Cottage, Liz texted Kevin to tell him to let Tilly know she should go there when she was free. Then all they could do was wait. Niall made lunch.

'This is a disaster,' sighed Liz, pushing a tomato round her plate.

'She's going to have a hell of a time proving the tools aren't hers,' said Benedict. 'Seb Galloway will have his work cut out.'

'How good is he?' asked Niall. 'Have you used him before?'

'No, actually. Connie recommended him. In fact, she introduced us the other night.'

Liz frowned. 'The other night?'

'In York.'

She tried to mask her surprise. She had no idea Constance had been at the Castle Museum benefit. Benedict had stayed in York overnight. Had Constance stayed over too?

With difficulty, she tore her train of thought from Constance to the matter at hand.

'It had to be Stevenson who planted the tools. He thinks Tilly set Flint on him.'

'They're not bf's, that's for sure,' agreed Niall. 'They had a square-go at the football.'

'Football?' asked Benedict.

Liz explained. 'We went to see Whitby Town on Saturday morning.' She paused, then added, 'While you were in York.'

'Odd that you didn't mention it.'

Just like you didn't mention Constance was at the benefit. Liz didn't voice that thought, but made an non-commital noise instead.

Benedict checked his watch. 'I really have to get to work. They'll be thinking I've abandoned them.' He stood up and got his jacket. 'Thanks for lunch, Niall.'

Liz followed him to the door.

'Call me later, won't you?' He kissed her cheek. 'Let me know when Tilly gets out. Keep me in the loop.'

IT WAS ALMOST seven o'clock when Tilly eventually knocked at the door. Niall was working his shift at the Duke of York. He hadn't wanted to go, but Liz had insisted, so Liz was on her own. She let Tilly in and hugged her.

'You look exhausted.'

'You would too, if Flint had grilled you for nine hours.'

'I was beginning to think you might not get bail.'

'So was I. But in the end they only charged me with breaking and entering. Seb insisted they have no evidence to link me to Christian's death. I dare say Flint's working on that.' Tilly looked around, as if she wasn't quite sure where she was.

'Why don't you go and have a shower, while I make you

something to eat?' suggested Liz. 'Your things are in the spare room.'

'How was Mags?'

Liz pulled a rueful face.

'She thinks I did it, doesn't she?' Tilly sighed and ran a hand through her cropped hair. 'You know what? Fine.'

'Fine?'

'I thought she knew me, but she clearly doesn't. And it's exhausting. Constantly having to prove myself, like I'm always on probation.'

'Don't be too hard on her,' pleaded Liz. 'You have to admit, police finding the tools in the café looks bad.'

'Bloody Snaky,' spat Tilly. 'I'll kill him if I get my hands on him.'

'You definitely think he did it?'

'Who else could it be? Who else could have got in and out of the café without leaving any trace? It was a professional job.'

'Just like the gallery.'

'Exactly like the gallery,' agreed Tilly. 'I need you to promise me something, Liz. Promise you'll help prove Snaky is behind all this.'

'I promise.'

THE NEXT MORNING, while Tilly was having a lie-in, Liz took Nelson out for his walk then spent some time on her laptop. Dennis's nefarious activities were apparently tangential to the break-in at the gallery and the death of Christian Petit, but Liz knew he'd faked the painting of *The Rockpool* that had been swapped at some point for the real one.

She did an online search for Fassbender Dry Art

Pigments, and found that they were indeed a paint supplier, as she expected, but one that specialised in eighteenth century pigments. Which was odd, because the original *Rockpool* had been painted in the sixties. While she was online she delved deeper into Dennis's life. Several pages into the results she found a paparazzi photo of him getting out of a car with a woman. Liz recognised her immediately as the woman in the polaroid photograph she'd seen in his studio. She read the caption – *Star of* Far From the Madding Crowd *arrives at the premiere with a friend.* Liz had to laugh at herself. She'd thought the woman in the polaroid might have been a clue, but it was Julie Christie. There was no way she had anything to do with the break-in at the gallery. It was actually quite funny. But it was another dead end.

She logged off, disheartened. Perhaps Dennis and the fake painting were red herrings? She should be concentrating on Snaky Stevenson. His alibi was bogus, but how could she prove it?

When Tilly got up, she looked as if she hadn't slept at all. There were dark hollows under her eyes, and her face was slack with fatigue.

'Bad night?' asked Liz.

'You could say that.' Tilly looked around. 'No Niall this morning?'

'He's gone to college. Can I make you some breakfast?'

Tilly shook her head. 'I feel a bit sick. Like I might be coming down with a migraine.'

'Hardly surprising.'

'My migraine tablets are at home... at the café.'

'I'll go and get them for you.'

· · ·

MAGS WASN'T in the café, but Gryzna let Liz into the flat to find the tablets. They were exactly where Tilly had told her they would be – in the bathroom cabinet. On her way out, she saw Skipper, sitting in his usual spot with the newspaper. His blue eyes widened when he saw her.

'Not stopping?' he called.

Liz shook the bottle of pills. 'Got to get these to a patient.'

'That's a shame.'

It was. Skipper must have seen the thought on her face because he grinned.

'If you come back,' he said, 'I'll buy you cake.'

Liz returned his grin. 'In that case, I'll see you in ten minutes.'

When she returned to the café, there was a steaming pot of tea and an almond crossant waiting for her at Skipper's table.

'I told him it was your favourite,' said Gryzna. She looked harassed.

'Any sign of Mags yet?' asked Liz.

Gryzna shook her head. 'Whatever kind of row she and Tilly have had, they'd better sort it out soon. The school holidays start tomorrow, and I cannot manage here on my own *and* look after my boys.' Her ten-year-old twins – Eryk and Lukasz – were a notorious handful. 'Would you like jam with your croissant?'

'No, thanks, I'm fine.' She took a seat opposite Skipper.

'Greek God of the sea. Second letter O, ending O, N.'

'Poseidon.'

'Thanks. I've been stuck on that for a while. You either know your Greek myths or you don't.'

'And you don't?'

'Definitely not.' He laughed, showing white, even teeth.

Liz stared at him. He looked rather like Neptune himself, with his big physique, beard and sun-tanned face. She shook the thought away. There was something she had to say to him.

'I have an apology to make.'

'Oh?'

'I'm sorry I interrupted you and Juliette the other day. If I hadn't she might have heard you out.'

'I doubt it.' He pulled a regretful face. 'It was a relief when you turned up, to be honest. She was giving me a hard time. Can't say I blame her.'

'It's not your fault, Skipper.'

'Johnny.'

'Sorry?'

'My real name is Johnny. You can call me Johnny if you like.'

'Erm... okay. Johnny.'

He gave her an odd look. 'I take it you've been looking into Christian's death?'

'What makes you think that?'

He just gave her a knowing look.

'Okay, I admit it.' She looked around to make sure nobody could overhear them, and dropped her voice. 'In fact... I think I know who broke into the gallery.'

'Who?' He leaned forward.

She hesitated. But she knew she could trust him. 'Snaky Stevenson.'

'Ooof.' Skipper made a noise. 'You need to be careful there.'

'You know him, then?'

'I do. He's not someone you want to tangle with.'

'He definitely did it. But he has an alibi for the night of

the break-in. Said he was playing poker with his friends. I'm going to ask them about it. Do you know who they are?'

'Seriously?' He leaned back in his chair and stared at her. She nodded.

'There's no way I'm going to tell you who he hangs out with. They're hardly going to confess the alibi is bogus, are they? And then you'll be on Stevenson's radar.'

Liz saw he had a point. Being on Stevenson's radar was something she should probably avoid, as Tilly had discovered. Skipper watched her as these thoughts played out on her face.

'Honestly, I wouldn't,' he added. 'Too risky.'

Liz nodded. He was right. She couldn't just go marching in, demanding the truth. She needed a better plan.

He turned his attention back to his crossword. 'Clean slate. Two words, first word five letters ending in K, second word six letters, third letter N, last letter S.'

Liz thought about it half-heartedly. If she couldn't bring Stevenson's alibi into question, then how was she going to prove he was involved? *Clean slate. Two words.* Could she provoke a confession and secretly record it? *First word ending in K.* Or somehow get Kevin to listen in? It was a tactic that had worked for her in the past. *Last letter S.*

She stared, startled, at Skipper.

'What?' he asked, equally surprised. 'What did I say?'

14

———

There was nothing for it: she was going to have to consult Constance, who was the only art expert she knew. Liz sighed. She'd rather not do that, but her conviction that Dennis's forgeries were somehow connected to the break-in and his death was getting stronger and stronger. After she'd left Skipper at the café (she couldn't really think of him as Johnny), she returned home to find Tilly had gone back to bed. That gave Liz some time to think, and to go online again. She searched 'art fakes' online, and learned a lot. Most interestingly, she discovered that art forgeries were often overpainted on original canvases of a similar period and size, bought or stolen specifically for that purpose.

Ironically, it was the crossword answer that had given her the clue. *Clean slate. Two words, first word five letters ending in K, second word six letters, third letter N, last letter S.*

Blank canvas.

It had reminded Liz about the canvas she'd seen at Dennis's studio. The stretchers and frame had clearly had some age to them, but the front had been prepped for repainting. Dennis had also been buying eighteenth-century pigments. Why would he do that, unless he was faking an eighteenth-century painting? Liz wondered about the label she'd seen on the back. It had the number 241 and the name Weston printed on it. She needed to consult an art expert. Which meant Constance.

Or did it? Liz realised that Constance wasn't, in fact, the only art expert she knew.

She settled Nelson in his basket with a treat, and headed out again. There was no question of taking him on this particular mission.

As head curator of the Abbey Museum, Dora Spackle was well-versed in art history and conservation. She lived in Anchor Cottage on New Way Ghaut, a narrow passage that was accessed by a tunnel with an iron gate just off Church Street and ran parallel to it, between it and the sea. About two thirds of the way down the alley, Liz turned down a narrow path to her left. Anchor Cottage was huddled underneath a red-brick extension of the Board Inn, which fronted on Church Street. Unlike the other cottages on the Ghaut, which were all eighteenth century, it was a nineteen seventies building made of red brick, with a plain door and no decorative touches. Liz marched up the path, took a deep breath and knocked on the door.

She had to knock twice before she heard movement inside and the door opened.

'Hello, Dora.'

Dora's eyes behind her spectacles narrowed and flickered to Liz's feet. 'You haven't got that dog of yours with you, have you?' Nelson and Dora had an ongoing feud that had started with a handbag and a kick that had – thankfully – missed.

Now they were arch enemies. 'What do you want?' asked Dora suspiciously.

'I just need to ask you a couple of questions. About art.'

'Art?' Dora snorted, then smirked. 'Oh yes, I forgot you were an art fan.'

Liz ignored the jibe. 'Can I come in?'

'I suppose.' Dora led the way into her kitchen, which was seventies style and almost entirely brown – brown units, brown lino, brown appliances. She indicated Liz should take a seat at the table, but made no move to offer her tea. 'What is it you're poking your nose into now?'

'Dennis's death.' Liz thought it best to keep things simple and not mention the gallery break-in.

Dora looked sombre. 'A terrible way for anyone to go. In a lavatory.'

The *Whitby Bugle* hadn't published that particular detail, but the town grapevine was very efficient.

'Did you know Dennis was an art forger?' asked Liz.

'Of course. Everyone did. He made no secret of it.'

'Would it surprise you to hear he was still forging paintings?'

'I wouldn't have an opinion on it one way or the other. None of my business.' She gave Liz a pointed look.

Liz felt irritation flare. 'Just like my posing for Dennis's class was none of *your* business. But that didn't stop you from going out of your way to tell everyone, did it?'

Dora sniffed. 'Is that what this is about?'

'No.' Liz realised she was getting off track. 'Have you ever heard the name Weston connected with art?'

'Weston?' Dora frowned.

'Yes. Connected with art.'

'What kind of art?'

'I don't know. Just generally. A dealer? A collector? An auction house?'

Dora frowned, thinking. 'Do you mean Westonbirt?'

Liz thought about it. Was it possible that label had partly worn off?

'Maybe,' she said. 'Who's that?'

'Lord Westonbirt was a Victorian collector.'

'And he collected paintings?'

'He collected everything. Paintings, sculptures, curios. It's all at Boosbeck Hall near Guisborough. It's owned by the National Trust now.'

Liz was silent. Guisborough was only about twenty miles away. 'I don't suppose you know if they've had a break-in lately?'

Dora frowned. 'Not that I know of. Why?'

WHEN LIZ GOT BACK to Gull Cottage, Tilly was up and about, making herself breakfast.

'Mags called,' she told Liz glumly. 'She wants me to go and get the rest of my stuff.'

'All of it?'

Tilly nodded.

Liz tried to hide her own dismay. Even though it was the largest of her two cottages, Gull was still snug for her and Niall, and would be snugger still with Tilly in residence. She could install Tilly or Niall in Kipper Cottage next door, but really needed the income from guests like Mr Kep.

Her thoughts must have shown on her face, however, because Tilly frowned.

'I'm so sorry, Liz. I should look for somewhere else.'

'Don't be daft. We'll manage.'

She saw Tilly's relief. Non-holiday rental properties were like hen's teeth in the town, and the few that *were* available were usually either run down or punitively expensive.

'I'm sure Benedict will let you keep some of your stuff at his place.'

Tilly nodded. They both knew that wasn't a long-term solution.

'How was Mags?' asked Liz.

'Determined.' Tilly's expression was bleak. 'She's pretty easy going most of the time, but once she's made her mind up about something...' Tilly's eyes filled with tears. 'I think it's over, Liz. I really do.'

Alarming theft at National Trust property.

Thieves caused thousands of pounds of damage to historic Boosbeck Hall after stripping the last remaining pieces of lead from one of the building's roofs. The theft was followed only a day later by someone breaking into the National Trust Property, near Guisborough, and stealing £50 from its café.

The lead was taken from the roof of a grade II listed building at the side of the hall that was once the servants' quarters and is now a gift shop and tearoom, last Thursday evening. Staff and volunteers only noticed something was wrong yesterday, when heavy rain led to water streaming through the damaged roof. Temporary repairs will now be made to protect the building from the elements, while the Trust decides how to find a more permanent solution. Lead has previously been stolen from the main hall roof, and the site is now without any of its

*original roofing material. Possible replacements could
include materials less attractive to thieves, such as stainless steel.*

*General manager Jessica Westonbirt said: "We had to put
the buckets out when it was raining, and it's now a rush to
repair the damage as soon as possible. We've stayed open
– this isn't going to stop us, but the cost of the damage is
going to run into several thousand pounds, which of
course takes money away from conservation work. Some
of this will be covered by insurance but there's quite a
large excess." Police are investigating. Anyone with information should call 101 or Crimestoppers, anonymously.*

Liz read the article twice. She'd found it in the online
archive of the *Teeside Herald & Post*, dated 20th August the
previous year. It made no mention of any stolen art, just the
roof lead and the cash from the café. She couldn't imagine
Dennis would be interested in lead or petty thievery, but it
was a hell of a coincidence they'd had two break-ins, when
that was exactly what she'd been looking for.

She decided to pay them a visit.

15

'I need a wee.'

'No, you don't. Just keep your legs crossed.'

'I do. It's leaking out!'

'Don't wee in the car!' shrieked Lukasz.

'I have to!' yelled Eryk. 'I'm bursting!'

'Oh, for heaven's sake.' Liz swerved the car into a layby and killed the engine. 'We've only been gone fifteen minutes.'

Lukasz smirked at his brother. 'I told you not to drink all that orange juice at the café.' He gave Liz a knowing look. 'He has a baby bladder. The size of a pea.'

Eryk scrambled out of the car. Liz followed.

They were in the bleak and beautiful landscape of the North York Moors, with rough grassland stretching out in every direction, tinged with purple heather. There were no trees or hedges, a fact not lost on Eryk.

'There's nowhere to go,' he gasped.

'Just do it here, in the ditch.'

'But people will see!'

There were cars passing, in both directions.

'Turn your back to the the road,' suggested Liz. 'No one will see you.'

Eryk scowled, hopping from one foot to the other in agony.

'What's the alternative?' asked Liz.

Eryk threw his hands into the air. 'Okay. But don't look.'

Liz turned away as he undid his trousers and emptied his bladder noisily into the ditch. It was a lovely day. The sun felt warm on her skin and, over the sound of passing cars and Eryk relieving himself, she could hear the song of a skylark. She spotted it, a speck of feathers high in the sky above them. In the distance, on the horizon, she could see the distinctive sharkfin shape of local landmark Roseberry Topping.

She was glad to be out, but wished she hadn't made the mistake of mentioning her proposed trip to Gryzna that morning. Gryzna had begged her to take the boys.

'Please, Liz. It would save my life. They have only just started their summer holidays and they are already doing my head in.'

Liz knew Gryzna was under extra pressure because they were shorthanded in the café without Tilly.

'Please,' begged Gryzna. 'They will have to stay here with me all day otherwise. I will give you money for lunch and any other expenses.'

'Don't be daft.' Liz knew Gryzna struggled for cash.

'You'll take them, then?' Gryzna brightened.

Liz realised she'd been manoeuvred. But the thought of taking the twins into a stately home filled her with anxiety and not a little fear.

She snapped herself back to the present.

'Are you finished?'

'Almost.' He took another few moments, fastening himself up again, then hopped back into the car. Liz got into the driver's seat.

'Where are we going, again?' asked Eryk.

'Boosbeck Hall.'

'Cool. Does it have rides?'

'No, it's an old house, filled with art and antiques.'

'Sounds lame.' Lukasz caught Liz's eye in the rear view mirror and grimaced. 'Sorry.'

'There's a tearoom. And a park. With deer.'

'Reindeers?' asked Eryk, perking up.

'No. Just ordinary deer.'

'Oh.'

Lukasz saw Liz's expression in the mirror. He nudged his brother. 'It's better than sitting in the café all day, isn't it?'

Eryk agreed, briefly, but then they bickered for the next twenty minutes. Liz was relieved when, just outside the market town of Guisborough, she saw the brown National Trust signage directing them to Boosbeck Hall. They turned off the main road and headed down a long, tree-lined driveway with lawns on either side.

'It's massive!' crowed Lukasz when the house eventually came into sight.

It was. The main body of the house was Elizabethan, with mullioned windows, dark stonework and tall, ornate chimneys. There were later extensions to either side that Liz thought might be Georgian, but she wasn't an expert. The car park was surprisingly busy for a week day – Liz reckoned the school holidays were to blame. She eventually managed to find a space not too far from the main entrance.

'I want you to promise to behave yourselves,' she said to the boys.

'We always behave ourselves,' said Lukasz. He caught her eye. 'Almost always.'

They crossed the lawn in front of the house, where there were benches with people enjoying the sunshine and eating ice cream cones. Liz noticed an ice cream van parked discreetly to one side.

'Ohhh. Can we have one?' asked Eryk.

'Please.'

'You can have one when we come out,' said Liz. 'If you behave yourselves.'

Liz knew that bribery wasn't a perfect parenting tool, but there again, she wasn't their parent. Any port in a storm.

As they paid their fee at the cash desk, which was tucked into a corner of the impressive beamed entrance hall, Liz noticed the typeface on the signage was the same as the label on the back of the canvas she'd seen at Dennis's studio.

'How old are the boys?' asked the elderly lady cashier. National Trust properties were often staffed by retiree volunteers.

'We're seventeen,' said Lukasz.

'Ten,' corrected Liz.

'We have a deer management workshop starting soon, if they're interested?

'What's that?' asked Eryk.

'Well, we tell you all about our herd of red deer, and how we look after them.' She saw the boys were unconvinced. 'And you get to feed the baby deer.'

'Cool.'

'Can we do that?' Eryk asked Liz.

'I don't see why not.' She tried not to seem too eager, in

case they changed their minds. It was actually the answer to her prayers.

'It's in the stables,' said the cashier. 'Just follow the signs. But you'll have to hurry. It starts in five minutes.'

They just made it. A young woman in a Boosbeck Hall polo shirt ushered them all into the stable yard, where they were assailed by the scent of dung and straw.

'Blerk!' Lukasz nipped his nose.

'It honks.'

Liz ignored them. 'How long does this last?' she asked the young woman.

'About fifty minutes.'

'Is it okay if I leave them here with you while I look around the house?'

The young woman looked at the boys. 'I should think so. You seem well behaved, don't you?'

The boys nodded, wearing their most cherubic expressions.

Liz legged it before the masks slipped. She headed straight back to the cashier's desk.

'Can I speak to someone in charge?'

'Is there something wrong?'

'No. I just need some information.'

'What kind of information?'

Liz realised she needed more leverage. 'I'm from the insurance company.' As soon as the words were out of her mouth, she regretted it. What on earth had made her say that?

'Oh. I think our estate manager Jessica is in today. Let me check.'

The cashier went out a curtained doorway behind the

desk, and returned a couple of minutes later. 'She says I should take you through.'

The woman led Liz through the curtain, and then took her down a long corridor, where the walls and doors were all painted Georgian drab. One of the doors was open. The woman showed Liz inside a small office that had a lead-paned window looking out over the lawns, a Victorian mahogany desk and a couple of claw-footed chairs. One of the chairs was occupied by a well-put-together woman in her forties, wearing a classic white shirt. Liz suddenly remembered her name from the article in the Teeside Herald & Post.

'Mrs Westonbirt.' She surmised that she was a member of the family who had originally owned the house, an ancestor of the collector Lord Westonbirt.

'*Ms* Westonbirt,' the woman corrected her, stood up and shook her hand. She cast a doubtful eye over Liz's jeans and sweatshirt. 'I didn't know Readman and Fletcher was sending anyone today.'

Liz deduced that must be the insurance company. She was in deep water... way too deep to back out.

'It's an impromptu visit. We just want to ask you a couple of questions about the break-in last year.'

'Is there a problem with the paperwork?' The woman forced a smile. 'You don't want your money back, do you?'

'Ha, ha.' Liz forced a laugh. 'No, not at all. Just firming up some of the details.'

'Please, take a seat.'

Liz sat in the other claw-footed chair, and felt the weight of the other woman's expectant gaze on her. 'Um... can you confirm the cash was taken from the café the day *after* the lead was stripped?'

'Yes. Someone broke in through the window in the game-larder on the ground floor. An opportunist... But you know that, don't you?'

'Of course.' Liz shifted uncomfortably in her seat. 'But I was wondering... *we* were wondering... it is a little strange that someone would break in, only to steal some petty cash. Is it possible the petty cash was just a diversion, that there was another theft you're not aware of?'

Jessica Westonbirt frowned. 'I don't understand.'

'Did you check your art inventory after the break-in?'

'There was no need. The break-in was confined to the café.'

'But isn't it still possible the thief who took the cash also took a painting? One maybe not on display, but in your archive? Something you wouldn't necessarily miss?'

'I'm sorry.' The other woman folded her arms. 'I'm not sure where you're going with this.'

Liz realised she had to come clean, or at least, *partly* clean. 'A painting has recently been found with one of your stickers on the back. And a number – 241.'

'Really?'

'Yes. I... *we*... thought we should check with you.'

Jessica Westonbirt went to the bookcase and took a large file from the shelf. It was dusty and clearly hadn't been looked at in a while. She put it on the desk to search through it.

'Here we go. 241. A late eighteenth century oil – *Leonidas the Third* – by Daniel Clowes. One of a pair. Twenty inches by sixteen inches.' The black and white photograph beside the description showed a portrait of a horse. Liz pictured the canvas in her mind's eye. The size was about right.

'It's in our archive,' said Jessica Westonbirt.

'Are you sure?'

The other woman gave her a level look.

'Can we take a look?'

Clearly unhappy, Jessica Westonbirt led Liz out, back along the drab corridor and down a stone staircase into the bowels of the house. Liz looked at her watch. She only had five minutes before the boys would be finished at the deer workshop, but she could hardly dash away now. Eventually they came to a steel door. Liz noticed there was no lock on it, but when Jessica opened it, the seal gave with a little hiss. Inside, Liz could hear the hum of climate control. The room itself was ancient, with rough stonework and a vaulted ceiling, but the storage system was state of the art, consisting of rows of vertical mesh racks with handles. Liz could see the gilt edges of the frames stored inside.

Jessica Westonbirt marched down the row of racks, looking for the right one. She found it, and pulled it out. There was a beat of stunned silence.

'Oh, my God.'

16

'So how long did they keep you?' asked Benedict. They were in Benedict's kitchen, which was on the chilly side in spite of the season, because the big Aga stove was turned off.

'About five hours.' She'd had a devil of a job explaining to Jessica Westonbirt and Detective Spencer of the Teeside police why she'd been posing as an insurance officer. They were suspicious about how she'd known the horse painting had been stolen, even when she'd explained to them about Dennis and the canvas. It had turned out there were two horse paintings missing from the archive. Liz suspected that one was the blank canvas she'd seen in Dennis's studio.

'Detective Spencer rang me last night,' said Kevin. 'He's coming this afternoon to take a look. If it is one of the missing paintings, Boosbeck Hall will be glad to get it back.'

Liz pulled a face. 'I doubt it.'

'What?'

'I don't think they will be. From what I could see, all the paint had been stripped off it.'

'Why would they do that?'

'It's what forgers do to make sure the canvas and stretchers look right when they fake a painting – they use a canvas of the same age and materials. They strip it first.'

'Really?' Kevin looked bleak.

Liz hesitated. 'I don't suppose Detective Spencer said anything about me?'

'He said a *lot* about you. But we had a good long chat, and I managed to persuade him you're one of the good guys.'

Benedict ran a hand through his hair and looked at Liz. 'How do you get yourself in these situations?'

She shrugged. 'I just have a talent for it, I suppose.'

Benedict didn't even crack a smile. Kevin spotted his father's expression and changed the subject.

'What do you suppose Dennis needed the canvas for?' he asked Liz.

'I have no idea. But I've a feeling it's connected to the break-in at the gallery and Christian Petit's death.'

Benedict stood up abruptly and collected their empty mugs, every line of his body registering his disapproval. Kevin caught Liz's eye. Liz grimaced. Benedict clattered the mugs into the sink.

Kevin stood up. 'I have to go.'

'Are you in the car?' asked Liz.

'On foot. Why?'

'I'll walk with you.'

Benedict saw them into the hallway.

'Are we still okay for dinner tonight?' asked Liz. 'Niall's at the Duke of York, and Tilly's having a meet-up with Mags to talk café business. I can make us a salmon salad.'

'Great.' Benedict gave her a perfunctory peck on the

cheek as she left. She and Kevin headed down the garden
steps together.

'What's up with you and Dad?' he asked. 'Have you had a
falling out?'

'No... I don't know. He just seems on edge lately. My
sleuthing never bothered him before.'

'Must be something in the water. An anti-aphrodisiac or
something.'

It was true. Everybody was at odds – her and Benedict,
Kevin and Anna, Tilly and Mags. Maybe Venus was in retro-
grade or something? Liz didn't really think much of horo-
scopes but really wanted to believe all the current romantic
trouble was temporary.

'Have you spoken to Anna?' she couldn't resist asking.

Kevin shook his head.

'Don't you think you should? '

'What's the point?'

Liz sighed. 'Really? It's got to be marriage or nothing? I
don't understand you, Kevin, I really don't.'

Kevin looked bereft. 'Sometimes I don't understand
myself.'

'Do you miss her?'

'Of course I do.'

'Then do something about it.'

It was only a couple of minutes' walk from Bagdale to
Spring Hill. Liz left Kevin at the station and headed back to
the east side of town. The summer crowds were out in force
now that the school holidays had started, with people of all
ages thronging the pavements, moving at an infuriatingly
slow pace as they took in the sights of the harbour, eating ice
cream or chips. The huge herring gulls were also a constant
presence, taking any opportunity to steal food or scavenge.

Whitby Council had put up signs around the harbour warning people not to feed them, but it didn't stop visitors from throwing them food, which just made them even bolder.

Liz was about to cross the bridge when she heard a shout above the chatter of the crowd.

'Liz!'

It was Skipper, waving to her from the deck of the *Stella Mae*, moored to the fish quay. She turned back, along St Ann's Staith, to the railings on the quayside.

'Come aboard,' he shouted up at her, surrounded by coils of rope and netting. 'I've just boiled the kettle.'

'I can't. I have to get back to Nelson. He needs a walk.'

Skipper's big wolfhound lifted his head at the word. Skipper grinned at him.

'What do you say, Griff? Fancy a leg-stretch?' He peered back up at Liz, shielding his eyes from the sun. 'Mind if we join you?'

'Course not!' She realised she'd be very glad of the company.

Skipper hoisted the big dog around his shoulders and climbed the ladder to where Liz was standing. She noticed he did it without breaking a sweat.

'Right,' he said as he placed Griff on the pavement. 'Let's go and get Nelson.'

They crossed the bridge in the throng of pedestrians, Skipper and Griff slicing easily through the crowd with their loping gaits, and Liz hurrying in their slipstream. They cut down Sandgate, past the café. Gryzna spotted them through the window and gave them a wave. Liz waved back, and also waved to Eryk and Lukasz, who were sitting in one of the window seats. They ignored her.

'Ouch,' said Skipper. 'Someone's in the doghouse.'

Liz sighed. 'It's a long story.' The boys had been in a terrible mood when she'd delivered them back to Gryzna the night before, having had to hang around for hours while the police questioned her. It was partly because they'd been bored, and partly because they'd never got the ice creams she'd promised.

'A long story?' said Skipper. 'There's nothing I like better.'

She told it to him after they, Griff and Nelson had climbed the one hundred and ninety-nine steps to the abbey and found a spot on a bench looking down on the harbour. He scratched his beard thoughtfully.

'A canvas, eh? I wonder what Dennis intended to do with it.'

'I have no idea. But I think, somehow, it was connected with the gallery, and Christian either found out about it or was in on it.'

'What makes you think that?'

'Juliette says that Christian was happier in the days before he died. He said things were looking up for them.'

'Do you think he was blackmailing Dennis?'

'I don't know. I don't really see Dennis as a killer; do you?'

'Not really. I don't see Christian as a blackmailer either, if I'm honest. He'd been in trouble in the past but he was really trying to make a go of things here. He was a good lad, at the bottom of him.'

They were quiet for a long moment, with only the sound of seagulls and distant voices filling the silence. They stared down at the roofs of Henrietta Street and thought about Christian.

'Juliette's gone,' said Skipper.

'Has she?' That meant the coroner must have released Christian's body.

He nodded. 'Can't say I blame her.'

'Me neither.'

'Oh well. What's done is done, I suppose.' Skipper stood up. 'I'd better be making tracks. Me and the lads are going out again this afternoon.'

Griff and Nelson joined them reluctantly as they headed back to the top of the steps. Just as they got to Caedmon's Cross, Liz saw James Bullington's gallery assistant, Brian, coming up Caedmon's Trod with Mr Dandy, the odious little pekinese. She supposed the peke's legs wouldn't have been able to manage the steps. Mr Dandy growled when he spotted Nelson and Griff, so Liz just waved to Brian from a safe distance. As Brian waved back, however, Mr Dandy's lead slipped from his grasp. He scrambled to retrieve it, and would have succeeded, except the pekinese suddenly realised he was unfettered. He darted, like a hairy missile, towards Nelson and Griff, barking as he ran. Griff gave a great, deep-chested 'Woof!' in response and ran to meet it. Nelson yipped with delight, and joined the fray.

The resulting fracas was mainly sound and fury, with lots of alarming yips and snarls but no actual contact. It took a few minutes for them all to get their dogs back onto their leads, but when it was over they saw, with relief, that there was no damage done. Mr Dandy, unabashed by the bigger size of his two opponents, continued to bark taunts at them as Brian dragged him off towards the abbey.

'All okay?' asked Skipper.

'I think so.'

'I hope that lad's getting danger money looking after that dog.'

'From what I've seen of James Bullington, I doubt it.'

Liz and Nelson parted company with Skipper and Griff at the bottom of the steps. Liz's phone rang just as she was letting herself into Gull Cottage. She could see from the caller ID that it was Benedict.

'Hello!'

'Hi. Just a quick call, about dinner tonight. I'm sorry, but I won't be able to make it.'

'Oh, that's a shame.' Liz thought about the salmon steaks she'd bought from Mike Howson that morning. She'd never be able to eat them both. 'What's the problem?'

'Not a problem, as such. Connie's in town unexpectedly, and I've said I'll help her with a new auction catalogue she's working on. A rush job.'

'Oh.' That was a slap in the face. But Liz rallied. 'I can come and cook you both dinner at your place if you like? I know what you're like when you're working; you forget to eat.'

'That's a lovely offer, but I think it's best if we just crack on. We can get a takeaway at some point.'

'Okay, if you're sure.'

'Quite sure. See you tomorrow?'

'Yes. Tomorrow.' Smarting, Liz hung up. She was tempted to call Skipper and ask him if *he* fancied salmon salad, but thought that would be venturing into dangerous territory. She knew Skipper was interested in her – he'd asked her out a few months before – and she really liked him, but not romantically. As irritated with Benedict as she was, she shouldn't involve Skipper in their domestic drama. He deserved better.

Niall arrived home soon afterwards. As usual, he didn't

even take his coat off before heading to the fridge to investigate the contents.

'Fancy some salmon?' asked Liz.

'I only have forty minutes.'

'I can have it ready in twenty-five.'

Niall blew her a kiss. 'You're a star.'

Once he had whirlwinded through the cottage, gulped down his salmon dinner and left again, Liz settled with Nelson in the sitting room. Even though it was warm outside, she was chilly, thanks to the thick stone walls of the cottage. She toyed with the idea of lighting a fire in the inglenook fireplace, but opted instead for a blanket. After she stopped shivering she tried to read a book, but found she couldn't concentrate. She couldn't shake off the thought of Benedict and Constance 'cracking on' together. Would Constance stay over? She hoped not, but there was no way of knowing whether she had without asking him outright tomorrow. And she had too much pride for that. Perhaps that was the problem? Perhaps she and Benedict had hit their recent speedbumps because she was too self-sufficient, too guarded to be open and honest with him.

Making a supreme effort to turn her thoughts away from Benedict and her own shortcomings, she wondered how Detective Spencer's visit to Dennis's studio had gone. She hoped Felicity Kitson hadn't been too disturbed by it, or by the fact that her dad had been keeping in touch with his criminal connections. Any one of them could have broken into Boosbeck Hall and stolen the paintings to order. Any one of them could have broken into the West Cliff Gallery and murdered Christian Petit.

But still Liz kept coming back to the same question.

Why?

17

'So you're going to be back working in the café?'

Tilly nodded as she put on her coat. 'Even Mags can see there's no sense keeping me away when they're short handed. This time of year is our busiest.'

Liz was glad. If Tilly and Mags spent more time in each other's company there was a better chance of reconciliation. But Tilly read her thoughts.

'She's still determined to move me out of the flat. Wants me to do it this afternoon. I've checked with B and he's happy to let me store stuff at his place. I went round to see him last night.' She eyed Liz. 'There was a woman there.'

'Constance. They were working.'

'Mm.'

'What does that mean?'

'They looked very cosy. Shoes-off kind of cosy. I think he was a bit flustered at me turning up.'

Liz said nothing.

Tilly decided a change of subject was in order. 'I don't suppose you're doing anything this afternoon?'

'No. I can give you a hand if you like. I think Niall's free too. He doesn't have classes on a Wednesday.'

'I don't have much stuff. It won't take us long.'

'HOW IN THE name of God did you get all this into your flat?' wheezed Niall, as he manhandled yet another suitcase up Benedict's garden path.

'The flat's bigger than it looks,' said Tilly, who was following him, carrying a straggling cheese plant.

'It must be. It must be the bloody Tardis.'

Liz puffed along behind them with an outsized plush dragon and a carrier bag full of hair styling equipment – hair driers, tongs and heated rollers.

'What do you need this lot for, anyway?' she asked. 'You don't have hair.'

'I used to,' countered Tilly. 'I used to have a shoulder-length perm.' She shuddered. 'Can you imagine?'

Liz couldn't. Tilly really suited her cropped, bleached look.

Tilly examined the bulging carrier bag Liz was carrying. 'I suppose I could probably chuck this lot.'

'You could have done that before we moved it all,' grumped Niall. They'd already packed the café van twice, and there was still at least one more load left at the flat.

'We're almost done with this one, I think.' Benedict passed them, arms free, heading back to the van.

They carried the stuff up to a spare bedroom. Thankfully it was one on the first floor rather than any higher up, but Liz was still out of breath by the time they got there. She dumped the dragon and the carrier bag on the ever-growing pile.

Tilly picked up the dragon. 'This was a present from Mags,' she said wistfully. 'We bought it on a trip to Wales.' She gave the dragon a squeeze and put it with the rest of the stuff. Then she spotted something hanging on one of the knobs of the built-in wardrobes. A silk camisole top. 'This isn't mine.'

'Maybe it belongs to Constance,' suggested Liz.

'Who's Constance?' asked Niall.

'One of Benedict's friends.'

Tilly hung the camisole back on the doorknob. 'At least you know she slept in here.'

'Not funny, Tilly.'

'What's not funny?' asked Benedict, appearing with an armful of scatter cushions.

'Nothing,' said Liz.

'I was just saying to Liz,' said Tilly, picking the camisole up again, 'that this isn't mine.'

Benedict looked at it. 'It must be Connie's.'

'She slept over last night, then?' asked Tilly with an innocent air. 'Does she do that often?'

'Not often, no.' Benedict frowned and dumped the cushions on the floor. 'What are you, the sleep-over police?' He headed out again.

Liz made sure she'd heard him go downstairs before turning to Tilly. 'Stop stirring. It doesn't help.'

'You need to get a grip. She's muscling in on your territory. '

'She's what?' asked Niall, round-eyed. 'Who *is* this Constance?'

Liz ignored him and glared at Tilly. 'I hardly think you're the one to be giving relationship advice; do you?'

'Ooof,' said Niall, eyebrows raised. 'Stick the knife in there, why don't you?'

Liz scowled at him. 'Stop being such a drama queen.' She turned to Tilly. 'I really don't need your help. There's nothing going on between Benedict and Constance.'

Tilly raised a sceptical eyebrow.

Liz modified her statement. 'And even if there is, I can handle it myself.'

THE NEXT DAY, Liz went to Dennis's funeral at St Mary's. She persuaded Tilly, Iris and Dickie to come with her, just in case there was nobody else there. Tilly had taken some persuading, given her recent arrest for the gallery break-in, but no one in the church took any notice of her. Felicity's concerns that no one would turn up had been unfounded – there was quite a crush in the church's Gothic interior. Originally built in the 12th century, St Mary's had been refitted in the eighteen hundreds with polished wooden box pews and white-painted balconies supported by barley-twist posts. It had an unusual double pulpit with a carved canopy, and a beautiful stained-glass window that scattered jewelled colours over the people gathered inside. Liz saw a lot of people she knew, including Skipper, Mike Howson and his wife, and Dora Spackle.

The service was oddly upbeat, with several of Dennis's old friends and art school colleagues making speeches. Even one of his old prison warders read a passage from the Bible. It seemed that Dennis had made friends *everywhere* he went. Afterwards everyone headed out of the church to the Brunswick Centre, where Felicity had laid on lunch.

'IT SEEMS A BIT WEIRD IF YOU ASK ME,' bellowed

Iris, 'GIVING HIM A SEND-OFF IN THE VERY PLACE WHERE HE WAS DONE IN.'

Tilly and Niall exchanged a look of alarm and steered Iris further off the path.

'WHERE ARE WE GOING? I WANT TO GO TO THE DO.'

'We'll just wait here a minute and let everyone get down the steps,' soothed Tilly.

'LET EVERYONE EAT EVERYTHING, MORE LIKE. COME ON, DICKIE, OR THERE'LL BE NOTHING LEFT.' Iris and Dickie set off at a trot after the rest of the crowd.

'Do you think we should go with them?' suggested Niall. 'Stop her from getting into trouble?'

'Go ahead if you think you're up to it,' said Tilly. 'I have to get back to the café anyway.'

'Actually, I think I'll come with you. I need something proper to eat.' Niall was always hungry, but no matter how much food he shovelled into his skinny frame he never seemed to put on weight.

'What about you, Liz?' asked Tilly. 'Can I tempt you to lunch at the café?'

'I don't see why not... Hang on a minute.' She'd spotted someone else she knew, coming out of the church. She hurried to catch up with Angel and Skye Bullington as they headed down the path. Angel was dressed in black, complete with gloves and an old-fashioned veil, while Skye was wearing a pair of grey dungarees and a hat that looked like it had been stitched together from dishcloths.

'Hello!' said Liz, as she reached them.

'Oh. It's our patient with the nettle stings,' said Angel. 'How are you?'

'Very well, thanks, considering where we've just been.'

'Poor Dennis,' sighed Angel.

Skye rolled her eyes heavenwards, impatient with her sister's sentimentality. She turned to Liz. 'I managed to get him a mate.'

Liz blinked. 'Dennis?'

'*Cetonia aurata*. I found her on the internet. A mail-order bride.' She sniffed. 'The computer has its uses.'

'This is Tilly and Niall,' said Liz, as the others joined them. 'Angel and Skye Bullington.'

'Tilly?' repeated Angel.

'Yes. Mathilda Fairweather. But I prefer Tilly.'

'Oh dear.'

There was an awkward silence.

Angel explained herself. 'We heard you'd been arrested.'

'Thanks very much for reminding me,' said Tilly. But then she saw the concern in the old lady's eyes. 'It's all a misunderstanding.'

Angel took Tilly's hand and patted it. 'We know, dear, we know. Don't we, Skye?'

Skye Bullington gave her sister a warning glare. 'Come on. Less of the chatter. Our taxi will be waiting.'

'Oh. Oh, yes, of course.' Angel adjusted her veil, flustered. 'Got to get a move on. *Tempus fugit,* and all that. Bye!'

Liz watched as Skye steered Angel away down the path, towards the museum car park. Then they headed down to the café. As soon as Mags saw them she made a beeline for the kitchen and left Gryzna to serve.

'A SCONE FOR ME, PLEASE. BUT NO JAM, AS IT'S THURSDAY.' Iris had taken one look at the food on offer at the funeral buffet and had headed back to the café. She and Dickie had arrived just after Liz, Niall and Tilly. 'LIFE'S

TOO SHORT TO EAT STALE SAUSAGE ROLLS,' she'd declared. Everyone agreed she had a point.

Liz quietly stirred her tea as everyone decided what they wanted to eat. She'd asked Benedict if he wanted to come to the funeral but he'd had business at the museum. She suspected, however, that he was avoiding spending time with her, and that made her anxious. She really wasn't good at handling domestic drama. She didn't have the patience for it, or, if she was honest, the energy. Perhaps she should just ask him outright what was going on with him and Constance? They could discuss the fact they hadn't really been getting on and let the chips fall where they would.

'PENNY FOR THEM?' asked Iris.

'They're really not worth a penny, Iris. Believe me.'

'YOU'VE BEEN VERY QUIET TODAY.'

'Yes, well, we've just been to a funeral, haven't we?'

Tilly joined the conversation. 'We bumped into the Bullington sisters after you left the church, Iris. Do you know them?'

'I DO. AWAY WITH THE FAIRIES, THEM TWO. ALWAYS HAVE BEEN.' She tapped her forehead. 'THE WHOLE FAMILY'S NOT RIGHT IN THE HEAD. THE MOTHER CHUCKED ALL HER MONEY AWAY ON THE HORSES, YOU KNOW.'

She saw Tilly's chastising look.

'I'M JUST TELLING IT LIKE IT IS. YOU KNOW ME, I NEVER CALL A SPADE A SHOVEL.'

'Maybe you should try it. You might make more friends.'

'I DON'T NEED FRIENDS. I HAVE YOU LOT.' Iris took her tea and went to join Dickie, who was talking to Niall.

Liz couldn't help but laugh. But then she saw Tilly's expression.

'What?' she asked.

Tilly pulled a face. 'Didn't you think our conversation with Angel and Skye was a bit odd?'

'Odd, how?'

'Was it my imagination, or did Angel Bullington really seem to *know* I didn't break into the gallery?'

18

On reflection, Tilly had a point. It wasn't just Angel's evident concern for Tilly that had been strange, but also Skye's reaction to it. She'd given her sister a warning look that had clearly said 'Shut up!' and hadn't been able to get Angel away from them fast enough.

Tilly and Liz discussed it after everyone else had left the café.

'How would they *know* I was innocent?' mused Tilly. 'Do they know who's guilty?'

'Why would two old ladies get mixed up in an art heist?' As soon as Liz asked the question, the answer came to her – a vision of two children playing on the beach. '*The Rockpool*,' she said.

'The whatnow?'

'The picture that had paint thrown on it. The one that turned out to be fake. It was owned by James Bullington, Angel and Skye. What if the old ladies hadn't wanted their brother to sell it?'

'Mm. So why didn't they just tell James they didn't want to sell?'

'I think legally they would have to. As a joint legacy, if one of the parties wants to sell, the other parties either have to buy them out, or the sale has to go ahead. I think that's how it works. I doubt Angel and Skye would have enough money to buy James out.'

'But surely he wouldn't take legal action against his sisters?'

'From what I've seen,' said Liz, 'I wouldn't put it past him. There's clearly no love lost. Skye thinks he's an arsehole.'

'But having a forgery made, and arranging a break-in – that's a hell of a lot of trouble to go to, isn't it?'

'Unless you happen to be good friends with a master forger with criminal connections.'

Tilly's eyes grew round. 'Do you think that's what happened? Do you think the break-in was to swap the paintings?' She frowned. 'Why didn't they just give the forgery to James to sell?'

'I don't know. Maybe they couldn't risk him having it in his possession for too long, in case he spotted it? Maybe it wasn't ready in time?'

'So they got Stevenson to break in and do the switch? And he killed Christian? That would explain why they knew I hadn't done it.'

Liz frowned. It was certainly one explanation, but it still left some important questions unanswered. Why was Christian killed six hours *after* the break-in at the gallery? Was the Boosbeck Hall break-in connected, or coincidental? And who had killed Dennis?

'It's just a theory,' she said. 'We can't prove any of it.'

Tilly gave her an odd look. 'Are you sure about that?'

. . .

'YOU WANT ME TO WHAT?' Iris and Dickie were sitting at the table in the window of her room at the Anchorage Retirement Home, where they could watch the world go by on the promenade. Liz had just joined them, to put the first part of the plan into action.

'Invite Angel and Syke Bullington to lunch.'

'WHY IN THE NAME OF ALL THAT'S HOLY WOULD I DO THAT?'

'Because you know they're interested in the Anchorage.'

'ARE THEY? FIRST I'VE HEARD. WHAT'S THAT GOT TO DO WITH ME?'

Liz summoned all her patience. 'Because you thought they might like a look around.'

'I BARELY KNOW THEM.'

Liz played her trump card. 'And you'd be helping my investigation.'

Iris's eyes narrowed. 'WHAT INVESTIGATION?'

'Into Christian and Dennis's deaths. And the break-in at the gallery.'

'WHAT'S THAT GOT TO DO WITH THE BULLINGTON SISTERS?'

'It's a long story.'

Iris crossed her arms. 'YOU CAN'T EXPECT ME TO GET INVOLVED AND INVITE THEM INTO MY HOME WHEN THEY MIGHT BE MURDERERS.'

'They're not murderers.'

'HOW DO YOU KNOW?'

'Because I do.'

'SO WHY ARE YOU INVESTIGATING THEM?'

Liz finally gave in and told them both everything. When she'd finished, Iris pulled a face.

'WELL, THAT'S A CAN OF WORMS, AND NO MISTAKE.'

'You'll invite them to lunch?'

Iris shrugged. 'I DON'T SEE WHY NOT. BETTER THAN SITTING HERE TWIDDLING OUR THUMBS, EH, DICKIE?'

'Our what?' asked Dickie mildly.

'OUR THUMBS!'

Dickie nodded. 'Oh yes.'

'MIGHT AS WELL BE USEFUL, EH?'

'There is one catch,' added Liz.

Iris eyed her.

'You'll have to go to Robin Hood's Bay to pick them up and bring them here. You have a car, Dickie, don't you?'

Dickie nodded. 'My Jag. I don't often get it out of the garage for an airing.' Liz was surprised Dickie had such a high-end car, but then remembered he'd been quite a successful jockey in his day.

'OKAY, THEN. GIVE ME THEIR PHONE NUMBER AND I'LL CALL THEM.'

Liz passed Iris a piece of paper. She'd had to look at the online phone directory to get it.

'WHAT DAY DO YOU WANT US TO DO IT? IT CAN'T BE TUESDAY 'CAUSE I HAVE MY CHIROPODIST. AND YOU HAVE BOWLS ON FRIDAY, DON'T YOU, DICKIE?'

'Any day that suits you and that suits them. They might say no anyway.'

Iris gave her a look that implied they wouldn't dare.

.   .   .

IT TURNED OUT, they didn't. Quite what they'd thought when Iris rang them up out of the blue and bellowed her invitation, Liz had no idea. But it must have been effective, because a date was set for Angel and Skye to visit the Anchorage on the following Monday.

Liz met Tilly at the appointed time in Tin Ghaut car park where she kept her car. To her surprise, Tilly was empty handed.

'Aren't you taking anything with you? Any tools?'

'Are you mad?' said Tilly. 'Can you imagine what would happen if the police caught me going equipped? They'd revoke my bail and throw the book at me. I'll just improvise when we get there.'

They drove to Robin Hood's Bay mostly in silence, both preoccupied with their own thoughts. Liz was thinking about Benedict. They'd spent Sunday together, and he had even stayed the night. On the surface, everything was as it used to be, but Liz wasn't happy. She'd sensed a reservation under the surface – a holding back – that hadn't been there before. She decided she needed to speak up about it, even if it risked driving Benedict away.

When they got to Robin Hood's Bay they parked in the car park at the top of the hill and waited. Liz saw Tilly's grim expression.

'Mags wouldn't be happy if she knew about this, would she?' she said.

'She's not happy now,' said Tilly, 'so what's the difference? I can't just sit around waiting for Flint to stitch me up. I have to prove it was Snaky.'

Liz could see her point. Just then, her phone pinged. It was a text from Iris.

THE EAGLES ARE OUT OF THE NEST.

All in upper case. Liz had to laugh – Iris even texted at full volume. She showed the text to Tilly. 'I think that means they've picked up Angel and Skye.'

Tilly looked at her watch. 'We have about an hour, I'd say. Shall we go?'

They walked down through the village to the Smugglers' Inn and turned right. A few minutes later they'd reached the gate at the end of the track, with its sign.

MARNAR DALE HOUSE. STRICTLY PRIVATE. NO NOSY PARKERS.

Liz took a deep breath as they went through the gate. At the end of the tangled track Tilly got her first view of the house. With its crooked chimneys and the compound eyes of the mullioned windows, it reminded Liz of a crouching bug. Tilly gave a low whistle. 'Quite a place.'

'You can see why it's too much for them.'

Tilly regarded it with business-like determination. 'Let's see if they've left a window open,' she said. 'You take the front, I'll go round the back.'

Liz wasn't particularly happy to split up, but she could see the wisdom of it – it meant they could get in and out faster. She scouted the front of the house. Everything was silent, almost expectant. It reminded her of Walter de la Mare's poem, "The Listener".

'Is there anybody there?' said the Traveller,
  Knocking on the moonlit door;

And his horse in the silence champed the grasses
Of the forest's ferny floor...
But no one descended to the Traveller;
No head from the leaf-fringed sill
Leaned over and looked into his grey eyes,
Where he stood perplexed and still.

Liz shook off her fancifulness, and inspected the windows. All the windows on ground level were closed. She stepped back to take a look at the ones on the first floor, overhung with ivy, but couldn't see anything open. She turned her attention back to the ground floor, and almost jumped out of her skin.

Tilly's face, as pale as Catherine Earnshaw's ghost, glimmered at her through the leaded glass of one of the windows. Liz put her hand to her chest to steady her thumping heart.

'The back door wasn't locked,' shouted Tilly. 'Go to the front door and I'll let you in.'

Liz did as she suggested, and Tilly let her into the cluttered hallway. Liz took a deep breath to soothe her nerves. Now they had crossed the Rubicon – there was no going back. Tilly looked around at the stacks of chairs, broken mirrors, bicycles, and books.

'Where the hell do we start?' she muttered.

'I don't know,' said Liz. 'Where would you keep something you didn't want anyone else to see?'

'Good point. Not downstairs, probably.'

They climbed the staircase at the back of the hall, picking their way through piles of books on the stairs. As they did so, Tilly accidentally bumped a small glass tank that was perched precariously on one of the stacks. It slid, as if in slow motion, borne on an avalanche of books, until it crashed onto the stone floor at the bottom.

They hurried down after it. It was well and truly broken, and whatever it was that had been inside it, now wasn't.

'So much for a quick in and out,' said Tilly. She picked up the label that had been on the tank and read it aloud. '*THERAPHOSIDAE*. What the hell is that?'

'Whatever it is, said Liz, 'I hope it isn't hurt.' She stared in dismay at the shattered tank. 'Shall we clean it up?'

Tilly shook her head. 'They might think it slid down on its own. It was a daft place to put it.'

They climbed the stairs again. Upstairs there was a long landing, with a beamed roof and many doors leading off it.

'I'll start at this end,' said Tilly. 'You start at that one.'

The first room Liz tackled looked like a spare bedroom, and was stacked with cardboard boxes. Her heart sank – the painting could be in any one of them. But then she rationalised. If Angel and Skye had kept the real painting, they'd done it because they loved it. They would want to be able to see it. She guessed they didn't get many visitors, so it was probably hanging on a wall somewhere. That made the search easier.

The next room Liz looked in was exactly the same – piled with cardboard boxes. After that, she found a bathroom with stained Victorian sanitaryware, and then another bedroom. This one was clearly in use. There was a brass bed with a lilac lace bedcover that smelled of lavender, and bookshelves filled with dolls. Some were large china-faced ones, others smaller, but they all gave Liz the creeps, staring at her accusingly. She guessed she was in Angel's room. There were several paintings on the walls, but they were all portraits – more staring eyes. She peered quickly in the closet, which was full of clothes, and quite a few moths, then, just for the sake of thoroughness, she looked under the bed, where she found a lot of dust bunnies and a couple of battered vanity cases. Feeling guiltier and guiltier about her intrusion, Liz left them alone. They were too small to hold *The Rockpool* anyway. She went back out onto the landing, where she saw Tilly coming out of one of the other rooms.

'No luck?'

Liz shook her head.

'Me neither. Do you think we could be wrong? Are we on a wild goose chase?'

Before Liz could answer, they heard a sound – a sound very like the front door opening and closing again. They froze, and stared at each other, round eyed.

'Who?' mouthed Tilly.

Liz shrugged. They hadn't locked the door – it could be anyone.

They heard purposeful footsteps in the hall, and then the crunch of glass, presumably from the broken tank. Liz peeped quickly over the bannister and saw the top of a black-dyed head. She pulled back again quickly.

'Bullington,' she mouthed to Tilly.

'What's he doing here?'

Liz had no idea. But she couldn't imagine Angel or Skye would be happy about it.

'Where are you?' Bullington's voice rang out, loud in the silent house. 'Come out. I know you're here.'

Liz and Tilly stared at each other, aghast.

'Mrs McLuckie!' Bullington's tone was upbeat, almost jocular. 'I know it's you. Come down here, please. Let's not waste precious time.'

Liz realised she had no choice. She started down the

stairs. Tilly made to follow her, but Liz stopped her with her hand on her arm, and shook her head. If Tilly was discovered she would get into terrible trouble.

'Go,' mouthed Liz. It was possible that James Bullington might not know there were two of them.

Tilly nodded, reluctantly, but made no move as Liz headed downstairs. Liz flapped her hand at her. Tilly sped off down the corridor. Liz guessed it wouldn't take her long to find a way out.

Bullington was no longer in the hall when she got to the bottom of the stairs.

'Mrs McLuckie!' His voice came from a door that stood open on the opposite side of the hallway to the kitchen. She squared her shoulders and went in. She found herself in a large, beamed room with peeling floral wallpaper and two battered Chesterfield sofas. James Bullington was sitting, perfectly at ease, on one of them.

'There you are,' he said, crossing one impeccably tailored leg over the other. 'I saw you and your friend in the car park, and followed you. I guessed what you were looking for.'

'And what's that?' Liz tried to sound as nonchalant as he was.

'The same as me.' He pointed to the fireplace. Liz looked. There, hanging in full view on the chimney breast, was a painting of two children playing on the sea shore. The real *Rockpool.*

19

'W here's your friend?'

'Friend?'

'The little blonde. She was with you when you got out of the car.'

'I don't know what you're talking about.'

James Bullington shrugged. 'Makes no difference to me, my dear. I'm not really interested in your illegal activities.' He stood up and sauntered to the fireplace to peer at the painting. 'You know, I've never liked this piece. No finesse. Clearly the work of an uneducated eye. I have no idea why Angel and Skye are so attached to it.'

Liz felt a surge of dislike. 'You were waiting for them to leave the house? '

'Indeed I was. When Connie Threadwell discovered the painting was a fake, it didn't take Sherlock Holmes to work out what had happened. I knew my sisters were friends with Dennis, and I also know a leopard can't change its spots.'

'So what are you going to do?'

Bullington gave a chilly smile. 'I'm going to teach them that crime doesn't pay.'

Liz was aghast. 'Surely you're not going to turn them in to the police?'

They were interrupted, suddenly, by the sound of the front door opening again. Liz thought at first that Tilly had had to resort to exiting that way, but then she heard voices.

'It was really rude to make them turn around like that. Why did you have to be so bad-tempered with them?'

'I don't understand why the bloody woman shouts all the time. Does she think we're deaf? Or stupid?'

Angel soothed, 'I'm sure she thinks we're neither. It was nice of her, wasn't it, to offer to pick us up and show us around the Anchor–'

There was a long pause, presumably while the two women took in the shattered tank.

'What the hell...?' muttered Skye.

'We're in here, sisters dear!' called Bullington.

Both women appeared in the doorway. They stared first at their brother, and then at Liz, uncomprehending.

'What are you doing in here?' snapped Skye at Bullington. 'Find the phone, Angel. I'm calling the police.'

Bullington moved quickly across the room, and offered her his mobile phone. 'Be my guest. And while you're talking to them, perhaps you can explain this.' He pointed to the painting above the fireplace.

There was a beat of silence.

'Oh dear,' said Angel.

'You didn't even try to hide it,' said Bullington.

'Well, we didn't think you'd be barging your way in, did we?' countered Skye. 'Why should we deprive ourselves of looking at a picture we love just because you're an arsehole?'

She scowled at him, and then looked at Liz. Her forehead creased in a question.

Bullington answered it. 'I bumped into Mrs McLuckie ransacking your belongings. She'd also worked out what had happened with Dennis Kitson, and the break-in.'

'We didn't mean for anyone to get hurt,' said Angel.

'Hush!' urged Skye.

But Angel wouldn't be hushed. 'He was just supposed to swap the paintings around, not hurt anyone.'

'You tried to defraud me,' said Bullington.

Liz snorted. He was clearly more concerned with himself than with Christian's death.

'You shouldn't have forced us to sell it,' began Skye. 'Any decent man–'

'Any decent man would call the police right now, and... aaaaarrrrggh!' James gave a long, gurgling scream and leapt into the air. 'What is it?' he shrieked. 'Gerrritofffff me!' He did a frantic jig across the carpet. As he did, Liz saw what had caused his extraordinary behaviour – there was a huge spider sitting on the front of his trousers. Bullington whirled and flapped at his crotch.

'Careful!' urged Skye. 'Don't hurt her!'

But Bullington was past listening. He hoped from foot to foot, scarlet faced, and eventually managed to dislodge the spider. It hit the floor with a surprisingly loud *thwump* and scuttled off to hide under one of the couches.

Bullington glared at his sisters. 'You're mad!' he sobbed. 'Both of you. Just like Mother... You'll be sorry!' He ran from the room. They heard him slam the front door on his way out.

'There he goes,' sighed Angel.

'Gone to call the police, I expect,' said Skye. She saw Liz

glance at the sofa. 'Don't worry, I'll get her later, when she's calmed down a bit. He'll have scared her.'

'What are we going to do now?' asked Angel, wringing her hands.

'Nothing we can do, is there? Except fess up.'

Liz didn't know what to say. She'd never really thought much beyond clearing Tilly's name. Only now did it dawn on her that she couldn't implicate Stevenson without also implicating Angel and Skye. Even if Stevenson hadn't intended to kill Christian, the sisters had blood on their hands.

Skye saw the sympathy in her eyes.

'Don't feel sorry for us. It's entirely our own fault. It seemed like a good idea at the time, but we should have thought it through.'

'Can I ask... it was Stevenson who did the break-in, wasn't it?'

Skye nodded. 'We didn't have any contact with him, though. It was all arranged through Dennis. We couldn't believe it when we heard that poor security guard had died.'

'I don't want to go to prison,' sniffed Angel. There were tears in her eyes.

Skye said nothing. It was hard to imagine how they could avoid it.

'I have a suggestion,' said Liz. 'Let me call my detective friend. Tell him your side of the story first. Isn't it better to have a friendly ear now, rather than a hostile one later?'

Skye looked questioningly at Angel, who nodded. It made Liz wonder whether she should revise her assumption that Skye was the boss of the house.

Liz called Kevin and, while they were waiting for him, helped Angel to sweep up the glass from the tank in the hall.

Meanwhile, Skye rescued her tarantula from under the sofa and found her a new home. By the time Kevin arrived they were sitting in the kitchen drinking tea. Skye showed him in. He caught Liz's eye.

'What's going on?' he asked. 'You didn't say much on the phone.'

Liz looked at Skye and Angel, who gave her weak smiles. 'It's a long story, and not really mine to tell. I think I'll leave you to it.'

Fifteen minutes later, after a walk through the village, Liz found Tilly sitting at one of the picnic benches beside the car park. When she saw her, she jumped up and ran to clasp her hands.

'Are you okay?' she asked. 'What happened? '

Liz shook her head, still breathless from climbing the hill. 'I really don't know where to start.'

THE NEXT DAY, Flint dropped all charges against Tilly, and Stevenson was arrested for the break-in at the gallery. Tilly celebrated by buying Liz, Niall and Kevin a massive cheesecake. She didn't, however, call Mags.

'Aren't you going to let her know?' asked Niall, manoeuvring a huge piece of cheesecake onto his fork.

'I imagine she'll know by now anyway. It isn't as if news travels slowly round here.'

'So... what? You're waiting for an apology?'

'I think that's the least she can do; don't you?'

Liz sighed.

'What?' Tilly's tone was sharp.

'Nothing.'

Tilly put down her fork. 'Honestly? I'm wondering

whether Mags and I have a future together at all. She was so quick to jump to the wrong conclusion. She didn't hear me out when I told her I was innocent. Shouldn't a relationship be built on trust?'

Liz caught Kevin's eye, and he looked away. Tilly was right, and it was a lesson they could all do with learning. Perhaps she'd been too hard on Benedict. Too cagey with him. It wasn't as if she had anything other than a suspicion that Constance had him in her sights.

'This cheesecake's grand, isn't it?' said Niall, either oblivious to the undercurrents or deciding to change the subject. 'Where did you get it?'

'The Cornish Bakery on Church Street.' Liz turned to Kevin. 'Have you charged Angel and Skye yet?'

'Flint's still deciding what to charge them with.'

'But she will charge them?'

'I should think so.'

'And what about Stevenson?'

'Breaking and entering – of the gallery and the café. He's admitted to planting the tools there. We're also looking at the job at Boosbeck Hall to see if we can link him to that.'

'What about murder?' prompted Liz.

'We'll probably charge him with manslaughter for now, although he's denying he had anything to do with Christian Petit's death. He says he locked him in the upstairs bathroom, and that he was alive when he left.'

'What time was that?'

'About twenty-five past two, he says.'

'Which leaves almost six hours unaccounted for. Do you believe him?'

'Are you kidding? I don't believe a word that comes out of his mouth.'

'Have you asked him about Dennis's death?'

'He says he doesn't know anything about that either, and we don't have a shred of evidence to link him to it.'

'Pity.'

Kevin swallowed the last of his coffee and got to his feet. 'Go to go. Thanks for the cheesecake, Tills.'

'You're welcome.'

As Liz was seeing him out the door, Kevin dropped his voice so that Tilly and Niall couldn't hear.

'I was wondering... what's the best flowers for an apology?'

Liz grinned. 'Roses. Always. Lots and lots of them. You're going to talk to Anna?'

'I am. I've decided I don't care if she marries me.' He hesitated. 'Well... I do, obviously... but I'm happy to let things go at her speed. If she takes me back, I'm going to pull a sickie and take her away for the weekend.'

'Flint won't be happy about that.'

'Flint can lump it. I have to get my priorities right, don't you think?'

'I do.'

When Liz returned to the table she saw the cheesecake had gone. Niall patted his stomach. 'That was grand.'

'Do you think I could leave you two to do the dishes?' asked Liz.

'No worries,' said Niall.

Tilly collected their plates. 'Where are you off to?'

'I just need to run a few errands,' she answered vaguely. In the prevailing spirit of reconciliation, there was something she had to do.

.   .   .

SHE FOUND Mags in the kitchen at the café, making scones.

'You've heard the news?' asked Liz.

'I have.' Mags dusted the flour off her hands. 'How is she?'

'Relieved. And... if I'm honest... angry.'

'Angry?'

'With you.'

'Oh.' Mags sat down and rubbed her face, leaving floury smears. 'I suppose she has a right to be. But... you can see why I thought she was guilty, can't you? The tools...' she tailed off miserably.

'Stevenson broke in and left them here to frame her. She's done with all that, Mags. I honestly don't think she'll ever go back to her old ways.' Liz thought it best not to mention their adventure at Marnar Dale House. 'She thinks too much of you to do that.'

'You think so?'

'Definitely.'

Mags was thoughtful. 'Is she at your place just now?'

Liz nodded.

'Right.' Mags stood up and took off her apron. 'Tell Gryzna I'll be back as soon as I can.' She went out the back door.

Liz grinned. Hopefully that should do the trick. She went back into the café to give Gryzna Mag's message, and spotted Skipper at the counter waiting for a takeaway coffee. He looked bleary-eyed.

'Okay?' she asked him.

'Fine. I've just got back in. I need a shot of caffeine to keep me going for another couple of hours before I can go to bed.' He eyed her. 'What about you? You look very pleased with yourself.'

'Do I?'

'You do.'

'I suppose I am, quite. I've been playing Cupid.'

'Cupid, eh? The mischievous God of desire.'

She grinned at him. 'I thought you didn't know your gods,' she said, thinking back to their crossword of a few days before.

'Not as a rule, but I do know that one.' He gave her a look she couldn't quite interpret. He looked away again quickly, as Gryzna gave him his coffee. 'See you later.'

Liz stared after him as he went out of the door.

'All okay there, Liz?' asked Gryzna.

'Yes, fine.' A thought occurred to Liz. 'Actually, could I have two lattes to go, please?'

As the tide of reconciliation was running high, Liz decided to ride with it. She took the two coffees to the Captain Cook Museum, where she knew she would find Benedict at work. The museum was quiet, for the middle of the day. Benedict and Patrick were taking advantage of the lull to hang a new oil painting of the *Cutty Sark*. He was clearly surprised to see her.

'Is everything okay?' he asked, with a worried expression.

'I'm not sure,' she answered cryptically. 'Do you have five minutes to talk?'

He nodded, and ushered her into his office, where they both sat down. Liz gave him his coffee.

'I'm not sure where to start,' she said. She saw the look of concern in his eyes, and her heart gave a little thump. But she steeled herself. 'We haven't been getting on too well lately, have we?'

Benedict hesitated, then grimaced. 'I wouldn't put it that strongly, but... no, I suppose not.'

'Why do you think that is?'

'Honestly? I have no idea.'

'It wouldn't have anything to do with Constance, would it?'

'Constance?' He looked genuinely baffled.

'You've been seeing quite a lot of her lately.'

'You think...? Oh, my God, no. We're just friends. Old friends.'

They both fell silent. Benedict rubbed a hand over his face.

Liz pressed on. 'Was it our conversation about marriage? I'm sorry I blurted that out the way I did. The whole conversation sort of caught me by surprise.'

'You and me both.' He gave a rueful laugh.

'I'm sorry if I hurt you. I don't want to marry you, but that doesn't mean I don't want to be with you.'

'No, I can see that. I'd just... assumed... we were headed in that direction.' He shrugged. 'I'm not sure why I thought that.'

'I'm sorry.' Liz couldn't think what else to say.

'Don't worry, I'll get over it.' He saluted her with his cup. 'Coffee helps.'

20

The next day the whole of Whitby was agog with the news that Stevenson had been charged with manslaughter, and that Angel and Skye had been charged with being accessories.

'It just doesn't feel right somehow,' said Mike Howson, on his early morning trip to the smokehouse. 'Young Stevenson's always been a bit of a rogue, but I can't imagine him murdering anyone. As for the two old ladies, they're a bit eccentric, but everyone knows they wouldn't hurt a fly.'

'I take it no one's happy about their arrest?'

'That's putting it mildly.' Mike rubbed one of his red cheeks, and gave her a sideways look. 'A little bird told me you were involved?'

Liz made a non-committal noise.

'I just hope you know what you're doing, Mrs Mac. Because a lot of people think you've got it wrong this time.' He gave her a nod and continued on his way to the smokehouse.

Liz stood on her doorstep, listening to the clattering of crates as Mike delivered his fish next door. If she was honest, she wasn't happy about the way things had turned out either. There was no doubt, of course, that Angel and Skye had commissioned Stevenson to break into the gallery, but it was only to retrieve the painting their brother had essentially stolen from them. Like Mike, she also wasn't convinced Snaky was a murderer. It wasn't just that he claimed he'd left Christian alive, locked up in the bathroom, there was also that worrying six-hour discrepancy between the time he'd broken in and the time of Christian's death. There was definitely something else going on, she was sure of it. The question was, what?

She decided to take a day off, just for herself. After taking Nelson on his morning walk she took a cup of tea up to the sitting room and settled down to read some magazines. She'd always had a weakness for interiors magazines, particularly the ones that showed real homes – she'd found a lot of inspiration in them when she was doing up the cottages. There were half a dozen magazines she'd bought that she hadn't had the chance to open yet. She leafed through them, but in spite of the beguiling photos of cosy cottage kitchens and glossy bathrooms, she realised she was finding it hard to concentrate. It was unnervingly quiet in Gull Cottage now that Tilly had gone back to the café. The nagging feeling at the back of Liz's mind that things were somehow out of kilter persisted, no matter how she tried to distract herself.

She pushed the thought away, impatient, and reached for *Country Life*. It was a magazine mainly for the rich country set, but she sometimes bought it so she could daydream about the big houses for sale. She turned straight to the property pages. There were several houses that caught her eye, but one in Sussex particularly appealed to her. It had a pretty Palladian frontage, informally planted gardens and acres of land... She was interrupted by a sudden *BANG BANG* at the door downstairs, and Nelson's answering bark. She looked out of the window and saw two small, spiky black heads. So much for a day to herself!

When she opened the door, Eryk thrust a Tupperware box at her.

'Mum said we had to bring you this, to say thank you for taking us out the other day.' He scowled. She realised she still hadn't been forgiven for the way things had turned out at Boosbeck Hall.

She opened the box. It was carrot cake. 'Thank you. Would you like to come in?'

The boys looked at each other, unenthusiastic.

'I have ice cream in the freezer.'

The twins' faces brightened. But then Lukasz's dulled again. 'Mum said we had to go straight back to the café.'

'And no bloody messing about,' added Eryk, quoting Gryzna word for word.

'I don't think eating ice cream is messing about; do you? I'll text her and let her know where you are.'

The boys barged inside.

'What flavour ice cream is it?'

'Is it chocolate?'

'Do you have rum and raisin?'

'Or fudge brownie?'

'I like Phish Food too.'

'Fish food?' Liz wasn't sure she'd heard right.

Lukasz laughed, delighted. 'It's an ice cream flavour. Ben and Jerry's.'

'I don't have any of that, but I have chocolate chip. Is that okay?'

The boys made a fuss of Nelson while she scooped their ice cream into bowls and texted Gryzna.

'What's upstairs?' asked Lukasz, when she gave him his bowl. 'I've never been upstairs.'

'Do you have a telly?'

'Can we look?'

Liz nodded her permission, and they clattered up the stairs with their bowls of ice cream. As she made herself a cup of tea and cut a slice of carrot cake, she could hear them commenting on her furniture and – disapprovingly – the lack of a TV. There didn't seem to be much ice cream eating going on, but she knew the boys were accomplished multitaskers.

When she took her tea and cake up to join them, she found them ensconced on the sofa, leafing through her magazines, ice cream dripping down their chins.

Lukasz wiped his chin with his sleeve. 'I like this one.' He showed her the picture of the house in Sussex she had admired.

'Lovely, isn't it?' She took a seat in the armchair by the hearth.

'I'm going to have one just like that when I get married,' he declared.

'I'm not,' said Eryk. 'Mine's going to be bigger. I'm going to live in America. In California. I'm going to have a cowboy ranch.'

'They don't have ranches in California, stupid.'

'Yes, they do. Don't they, Mrs Mac?'

'I'm not sure, to be honest. They do have them in Texas though. And Arizona.'

'That's where I'll live, then.' Eryk nodded decisively. 'In Texas. And I'll have one of those huge Hummers and horses.'

'You don't know how to ride.'

While they were bickering, Liz picked *Country Life* off the floor where it had fallen, and looked at the house in Sussex. So beautiful, with a lake, and horses grazing in the paddock. So peaceful! Something tugged at her attention, and she looked more closely at the photograph. There were two horses grazing side by side, heads down on the lush grass. It made her think.

'...don't they, Mrs Mac?'

'Sorry?' She snapped her attention back to the boys.

'Cowboys wear knives on their boots, don't they?' repeated Lukasz.

'They do not,' scoffed Eryk.

'They're called spurs,' said Liz. 'I'm not sure they're used much now.'

'I hope not.' Lukasz shuddered. 'Poor horses!'

'I'm not going to wear spurs when I ride on my ranch,' declared Eryk.

The boys left forty minutes later, having eaten their own body weight in ice cream and most of her carrot cake. As she tidied the sitting room afterwards, picking up the magazines, Liz also tried to pick up her earlier train of thought. There had been two horse portraits stolen from Boosbeck Hall... but only one had been found in Dennis's studio. What had happened to the other one? It had been painted by Daniel Clowes, an eighteenth century artist. The receipts she'd spotted for paint had been eighteenth century pigments. Eighteenth century. She powered up her laptop, and found the West Cliff Gallery's online catalogue. Jessica Westonbirt had said the stolen horse portraits were twenty inches by sixteen inches.

Exactly the same dimensions as the portrait of Lady Henrietta Cholmey by Sir Joshua Reynolds.

21

'I'm just wondering why you printed that story,' said Liz.

Oliver Edwards, a big man with thinning hair and a broken nose that lent him a pugilistic air, grinned ruefully. 'It was just a balls-up, plain and simple. Young Bradley Harrison, one of my junior reporters, had a call from the gallery saying the painting was missing. Turns out, it was just some local idiot pulling his leg. It should never have made it into the paper. My fault, really. I should have fact-checked it, but we were only minutes from going to press. I didn't know we'd gotten it wrong until the gallery owner called me.'

'James Bullington?'

'That's the one. Lovely man.' Oliver's tone was ironic. 'We had a... lively... conversation. Quite a few of the nationals had picked the story up, and I had to spend hours ringing round, putting them straight. Let's just say young Brad will be writing up WI meetings and missing pet notices for the next few months.'

Liz thanked Oliver for his time and made her way out. Only a few years before, the building had been filled with the clatter of printing presses and the smell of ink. But now, in the digital age, it was much the same as any other other open-plan office, with phones ringing and people milling about.

The sun was shining outside, on the busy shopping street of Flowergate. Liz made her way home thoughtfully. Had the call to Bradley really been a prank, or had it been a deliberate attempt to mislead? If so, why would someone do that? Liz had no idea, but she was pretty sure she was onto something.

'So, LET ME GET THIS RIGHT.' Niall frowned. 'You think the Reynolds portrait in the gallery is a fake?' He was in the middle of making a papier mache something or other for a performance at college. The kitchen table was laden with soggy paper, chicken wire and glue. There were strips of paper everywhere – on the table, the floor, sticking to Niall's clothes and even on Nelson, who had – understandably – retreated to his basket.

'I'm pretty sure it is, yes,' said Liz. 'I think Dennis painted it.'

'Okay.' Niall scratched his nose thoughtfully with the end of his glue brush. 'But how does that fit with Christian's death?'

'I'm not sure. All I know is that there's more going on than there seems to be. Flint thinks she has her man now she's arrested Stevenson, but I'm not sure she has. I don't think Stevenson killed Christian. I think Christian found out about whatever was going on in the gallery, and that was why he was killed. And Dennis was a loose end that needed tying up. That's why he was murdered.'

'By?'

Liz hesitated. 'Well, the obvious suspect is James Bullington, isn't it? It's his gallery.'

'Does he own the Reynolds?'

'I shouldn't think so.'

'That's pretty key, don't you think? Either your man Bullington is trying to trick the owner, or he's trying to trick a buyer. Maybe he's in league with the owner?'

'I should think the owner's listed in the gallery catalogue.'

'Why don't you go and look, while I get this dragon finished.'

'Dragon?' Liz eyed the lump of soggy paper on the table. If it looked like anything, it looked like a chicken. A very fat, plucked chicken.

Niall glared at her. 'Yes. A dragon. He pointed at various bits of the lump. 'Those are its eyes, and that's its tongue.'

'Ah, yes. I see it now.'

Niall gave her a jaundiced look. 'Sure you do.'

Liz went up to the sitting room to look at the gallery catalogue on her laptop. She discovered that the Reynolds was owned by someone called Reginald Barton-Howe. After a bit more digging she found he'd attended the same private school as James Bullington.

When she came back downstairs she saw that the lump on the kitchen table had sprouted ears. It now looked like a plucked chicken with ears. Niall caught her eye.

'One word,' he said. 'One single word and I swear–' He broke off in despair.

'What's it for, anyway?'

'We're doing a performance of the *Hobbit*. I'm Smaug.'

'Ambitious. Is this to go on your head?'

Niall nodded. 'It's supposed to.'

Liz peered at the lump. 'I think you've made it too small.'

Niall threw his glue brush down. 'I've always been terrible at making things.'

His anguished expression tugged at Liz.

'Could you do with some help?'

His face broke into a grin. 'You're an angel.'

'I know.' She eyed the mess on the table. 'Let's get rid of this, shall we, and start again?'

THE NEXT MORNING, Liz made her breakfast around the results of their labours. The new dragon's head was larger and less lumpy than Niall's first attempt, and looked rather more like a seahorse than a dragon, but at least it fit on Niall's head. Niall thumped down the stairs and poured himself a mug of tea. He nodded at the dragon.

'Do you think it's dry enough to paint now?'

'I should think so.' She finished the last of her toast and went to put on her jacket.

'I can take Nelson out if you like,' said Niall. 'It's the least I can do.'

'I've already done that. I'm off to sound out the assistant at the gallery.'

'Sound him out?'

'See if he knows about any nefarious dealings.'

'You need to tread carefully.'

'Of course.'

Niall frowned, unconvinced. 'If you hang on five minutes and let me get some clothes on I'll come with you.'

'Okay, but hurry up. I want to catch him on his way into work.'

'HERE'S YOUR MAN.'

Just as they got to the top of the West Ciff, they spotted Brian's blue sports car turning into the Pavilion car park. Liz could see a smudge of orange – Brian's mop of hair – behind the wheel.

Niall put a warning hand on her arm. 'Let's not go charging in there. Whatever's going on in the gallery, he might have something to do with it.'

Liz shook her head. 'I don't think so.'

She waved to him as he got out of the car.

'Brian! '

He looked around to see where her voice was coming from, and spotting them, gave an answering wave. They hurried to join him.

'Mrs Mac. We keep bumping into each other, don't we? I hope your dog was okay after that business up at the abbey.'

'Nelson's fine.' She laughed. 'I think he was more surprised than anything that Mr Dandy had had a go.'

The conversation stalled. Liz plunged in.

'I don't suppose you have time for a coffee, do you? We want to pick your brains about something.'

'Erm... ' Brian looked at his phone, checking the time.

'It is rather important.'

'Okay. If we can make it quick. I have to open up in fifteen minutes.'

They took him to the Copper Kettle café, only a minute's walk along the promenade, and sat at one of the Art Deco style tables with their coffees.

'So,' said Brian, 'what's this about?' He gave them an uncertain smile.

'We just wondered whether you'd seen anything suspicious going on at the gallery,' said Liz.

'Suspicious?' His sandy eyebrows rose. 'Suspicious how?'

'We're not really sure. How well did you know Christian Petit?'

'Not at all. He'd only started at the gallery a couple of weeks before he died, when I was on holiday. I never actually met him.'

'What about Reginald Barton-Howe? Do you know him?'

'Of course. Reggie's an old friend of James's. And he owns the Reynolds. The portrait of Lady Henrietta.'

Niall shot Liz a warning look that she ignored.

'We think it's a fake,' said Liz.

Niall exhaled loudly. Liz was careful to avoid his eye.

'Fake?' Brian's glance flashed from Liz to Niall and back again. 'I don't understand.'

Liz told Brian everything. All about the stolen horse paintings, and the eighteenth century pigments in Dennis's studio, all about Stevenson's protestations and the worrying discrepancies in the timings of Christian's death. When she finished, Brian said nothing, just stirred his coffee.

'You don't seem surprised,' said Niall.

Brian just pulled a worried face.

'So, have you seen anything?' prompted Liz. 'Anything suspicious?'

'Not really.' Again, he paused. 'But this wouldn't be the first time James has been involved in something illegal. He once got into trouble for forging provenance on a painting. Back in the nineties, before he left London. A Paul Nash landscape, I think it was.' He shook his head. 'I thought it was just gossip.'

'No smoke without fire,' said Niall.

Brian frowned. 'Are you going to tell the police?'

'Not yet,' said Liz. 'We need to be sure it is a fake before we do that.'

'If it is, it's a bloody good one. It has everyone fooled. You'll need an expert to examine it.'

Liz just looked at him.

'Someone like Connie Threadwell.' He glanced at the time on his phone again and got to his feet. 'Sorry. I really do have to go. James will have my guts for garters if the gallery isn't open on time. Let me know if I can help at all.'

'Will do. Thanks.'

When he'd gone, Liz and Niall finished their coffees in silence.

'I really don't want to involve Constance,' said Liz, at last.

'I don't think we have much choice, do we? Not if we need an expert opinion.'

'She doesn't like me.'

Niall glanced at her, and caught her pleading look. He threw up his hands. 'Oh no! Don't look at me. I have a dragon to paint.'

'Liz. This is a... nice... surprise.'

Liz noticed Constance's hesitation over the word 'nice', and her guarded tone. Did she think she was ringing to talk about Benedict? She quickly disabused her.

'I'm sorry for calling you out of the blue like this. I wanted to ask you a professional question, about the Reynolds at the West Cliff Gallery.'

'The portrait of Lady Henrietta Cholmley?'

'That's the one.' Liz took a deep breath. There was no easy way to say it. 'Do you think it might be a fake, like the *Rockpool*?'

There was a long pause on the other end of the line, before Constance spoke again. 'You are pulling my leg?'

'No. Not at all. I think there's a good chance it's a copy. I think James Bullington got Dennis Kitson to copy it, using a stolen painting from Boosby Hall.'

'That's quite an accusation.' Constance's tone was frosty. 'You should be very sure of your facts before tossing accusations around like that.'

Liz chose to ignore the reprimand. 'Have you ever looked closely at it?'

'At the portrait? Not at close quarters, no. If it's a copy, it's a very convincing one.'

'Dennis was the best in the business. And Bullington has previous too.'

'James?' Constance was shocked.

'He was fined for faking provenance when he was working in London.' Liz had looked into it online since her conversation with Brian and had been able to confirm what he'd said. It hadn't been easy, because the affair had mostly stayed out of the papers, but the plaintiff had taken the case to the Sheriff court, and Bullington had ultimately been fined two thousand pounds. She told that to Constance.

'That's the first I've heard of it,' huffed Constance. 'And you should know there's a fine line between faking provenance and extrapolating evidence to draw the most likely conclusions.'

Whatever. Liz had no idea what she was talking about, and didn't want to be subjected to complicated, patronising explanations. 'I think the Reynolds is a fake, and that it has something to do with Christian Petit's death.'

'But they've caught the person who did that.'

'They only *think* they have. I'd like you to take a look at the Reynolds. A proper look.'

'How do you propose I do that? I can hardly just walk in there and demand James takes it out of the frame.'

'It has to come out of the frame?'

'It does. To be absolutely certain... And before you ask, I'm not prepared to go creeping around in the middle of the night like a criminal.'

'Don't worry, you won't have to. How soon can you get to Whitby?'

22

'N o! How many times do I have to tell you; the i's are harder, tighter... *circumstances.*'

'*Circumstances,*' repeated Niall. 'Better?'

Gryzna scowled. 'Not much. Your r's are shit too. No Russian would say them like that.'

'The accent doesn't have to be perfect,' soothed Liz. 'Just good enough to fool James Bullington.'

They were all gathered in the café. Tilly had closed it early so they could use it as their centre of operations.

'What if he recognises Niall when he sees him?' asked Mags.

'I don't think we need to worry about that,' said Niall. 'As far as I know, I've never met the man.' He was dressed in one of Dickie's tweed suits. It was old-fashioned, incongruous on a man of Niall's age, but it added to his air of foreign eccentricity. The look was further 'enhanced' by the addition of sideburns.

'HE LOOKS WELL DODGY IF YOU ASK ME,' opined

Iris, who had joined them in the café, not wanting to miss out on anything.

'Thank you.' Niall took a bow. 'I aim to please.'

'I still think I should do it,' said Gryzna. 'Why use a terrible fake Russian when you can have a real one?'

'You're not Russian, you're from Belarus,' countered Tilly.

'You think this man Bullington knows the difference?'

Liz had to admit she had a point, but it was too late now. James Bullington was expecting a Boris, and a Boris he must have. The café bell tinkled as someone pushed their way in. Constance dumped her suitcase and shook her dripping umbrella.

'I thought someone was going to pick me up at the–' She broke off mid-sentence, to stare at Niall.

He bowed and clicked his heels. 'Boris Morotzov, at your service,' he said in his best Russian accent. 'So pleased to meet you.'

'I don't think so.' Constance ignored his crestfallen expression. 'This is a serious business, not a pantomime.'

'BUT HE'S BEEN PRACTICING,' protested Iris.

'I don't care. My credibility is at stake. I'm not going in there with...' she flicked her gaze over Niall, 'a second-rate Bond villain.'

Everyone couldn't help but grin. Everyone except Niall, who scowled.

'What about Gryzna?' suggested Tilly.

Gryzna stepped out from behind the counter. 'I am from Belarus.'

Constance ran a critical eye over the statuesque redhead.

'Are you sure James hasn't seen you before?'

'I shouldn't think so. He has never been in the café, as far as I know.'

'We could say you're Boris's daughter, I suppose, and that he's been unavoidably detained. James has no idea how old he's supposed to be.' She pursed her lips critically. 'You're taller than me, and much heavier, but we might be able to find something in my suitcase to make you look respectable.'

Gryzna stared at her, stony-faced. Liz winced. Constance had no idea she'd met her match in Gryzna. As Tilly showed the two women up to the flat for the make-over, Liz prayed that Gryzna would bite her tongue. It would be a disaster at this point for Constance to back out.

While the two women were gone, Niall fumed.

'I shouldn't have to take this shit,' he muttered. 'I'm a professional actor.'

'A *trainee* actor,' corrected Mags gently. 'And if you're serious about the job, you'd better get used to rejection.'

'Was I really that bad?'

Mags smiled. 'I think it was the fake sideburns, more than anything.'

'CAN WE HAVE A BREW WHILE WE'RE WAITING?' suggested Iris. 'I'M PARCHED.'

As Mags went to make everyone tea, she caught Liz's eye.

'Are you sure we shouldn't go to the police with this?' she asked. 'Isn't it illegal?'

'I don't think so,' Liz reassured her. 'It's not as if we're trying to defraud or rob anyone. Just the opposite.' If she was honest, she'd have preferred Kevin to be involved, but after a successful reunion with Anna, he'd taken her away for the weekend. Liz was delighted they'd made up, even though it had left her high and dry. She certainly wasn't going to tell Inspector Flint about her suspicions.

Mags filled some teapots from the urn. 'Where's Benedict? Didn't he want to be here?'

'He had a meeting today,' lied Liz. She didn't want to admit that she hadn't told Benedict about the plan. She had a feeling he wouldn't approve. He'd find out about it afterwards, of course, but then it would be a *fait accompli*, and – hopefully – they would have uncovered Bullington's double dealing.

Constance re-emerged twenty minutes later, with a stranger in tow. Gryzna was wearing a green silk dress, her ears and décolleté adorned with gold. Her hair had been coiled on her head, and her face immaculately made up and finished with red lipstick. Everyone stared. Even Nelson lifted his head from his squeaky pig to look at her.

'May I present Galina Morotzov,' said Constance smugly.

'Wow,' said Niall. 'I've never seen you wearing make-up before, Gryz.'

Gryzna scowled. 'Yes, you have. Just not so much of it.' She glared at Constance. 'It itches.'

Constance ignored her complaint, and inspected Gryzna's hands, red from doing dishes. 'Pity we didn't have time for a manicure.' She sighed. 'Never mind. Let's get this pantomine on the road. James is expecting us.'

Liz, Iris and Niall took up their positions first, in the glass shelter on the West Cliff – a good vantage point to watch the gallery. Eryk and Lukasz were already there, having been collected by Skipper from school. They were part of Liz's Plan B, but Liz hoped it wouldn't come to that. Nelson greeted Griff, wagging his stumpy tail. Luckily, the rain had eased, so the boys were able to run around on the wet grass. It would have been quite crowded otherwise.

'Did you remember your binoculars?' she asked Skipper.

He handed them to her, and she focused on the gallery through the rain-spattered glass of the shelter. She was doing her best to hide how frustrated she was, not being involved in the actual operation itself, but Bullington knew her and would have been sceptical if she'd suddenly produced a potential Russian buyer for the Reynolds from nowhere. Constance, on the other hand, was above suspicion. Liz had to grudgingly admit they wouldn't have been able to do it without her. Once Constance had recovered from her initial shock, she'd shown a surprising commitment to the enterprise.

'Are you okay?' asked Skipper. He was standing close, a little too close, but Liz supposed that wasn't his fault. It was a bit of a squeeze in the shelter.

'Just a bit nervous. I hope this doesn't blow up in our faces.'

'I'm sure it'll be fine.' He patted her on the shoulder.

Liz blushed, and distracted herself by fiddling with the focus on the binoculars, until she'd got it just right. She could see most of the interior of the ground floor of the gallery through the window. James Bullington was pacing the floor, talking to someone just out of sight. Liz assumed it was Brian, who had been fully briefed on what was going to happen. She scanned the room, and spotted a gold-framed painting propped against the counter. Lady Henrietta Cholmey gazed demurely out, dressed in ermine and pearls.

Dickie's Jaguar pulled up to the kerb. James Bullington darted to the window of the gallery to look out, then darted back again. Liz couldn't see Dickie's face, but knew he was at the wheel, dressed in his best funeral suit. Constance and Gryzna got out, and Liz watched anxiously as they went into the gallery.

She saw Bullington greet them. He shook Gryzna's hand, so obsequious she thought for a minute he was going to curtsey. Then they talked. And talked.

'WHAT'S GOING ON?' demanded Iris.

'I have no idea.' It was so frustrating that she couldn't hear what was happening! Bullington lifted the painting onto the counter. Constance leaned over it, with her torch and eyeglass. She took a long time examining it, scanning it from top to bottom, before she straightened up again and said something to Bullington. Bullington shook his head. His demeanour changed.

Gryzna folded her arms and said something to him, but he shook his head again. Gryzna put one hand casually behind her back, where Bullington couldn't see it, and gave the pre-arranged signal: thumbs-up.

'That's it. Plan B!' hissed Liz. She clipped Nelson onto his lead. 'Eryk, Lukasz!' They stopped running about on the grass and scuttled to her side. 'You know what to do?'

They nodded, and took Nelson's lead. Everyone watched as the three of them skipped off across the grass towards the gallery.

'You're on,' said Liz to Skipper, who was still standing beside her. Still very close.

'Okay. Come on, Griff.' At the sound of his name, the big greyhound, forlorn at losing his playmate, looked up expectantly. They loped out of the shelter together.

Liz lifted the binoculars again, and held her breath as the boys and Nelson reached the gallery. As they got to the door, Lukasz turned and gave them a wide grin. Grandstanding. Then they went in.

There was a beat, two beats of silence, and then all hell broke loose. There was a flurry of barking inside the gallery, and the door crashed open. Nelson shot out, hotly pursued by a bullet of angry fur – Mr Dandy. Liz watched the door anxiously. After a couple of seconds, James Bullington crashed out after them.

'IT WORKED!' shouted Iris, gleeful.

Nelson bounded joyously around on the grassed area on the promenade, staying just a heartbeat ahead of the frenzied pekinese, while Bullington tried in vain to catch it. Then Skipper, from his position on the other side of the promenade, sent Griff into the fray, and the high-pitched yaps of the peke and the tenor tones of the bull terrier were joined by the bass notes of the greyhound.

Niall pushed Liz. 'What are you waiting for? Go!'

She hurried, head down, towards the gallery, passing less than thirty feet from James Bullington. Luckily, he was too occupied with the dogs to take any notice. He lunged to grab at Mr Dandy's collar as he flew past him, but his fingers only closed on air, and he crashed to the ground. Liz dashed into the gallery.

Constance snatched the tools she was carrying. 'You took your time.' She flipped Lady Henrietta unceremoniously onto her front, and started to prise her out of the frame.

'How long will it take?' asked Liz, breathless.

'Not long.'

Gryzna pursed her red lips. 'He said he wanted two thousand pounds to take it out so we could examine it properly.'

'I told you he would,' said Brian. He was twisting his hands, darting anxious looks at the door.

'Which is why we had a Plan B,' said Liz.

They watched Constance work. Brian was now hopping anxiously from foot to foot, making everyone else even more nervous. Liz put a gentle hand on his arm. 'Would you mind going outside? The more people we have out there making sure James doesn't come back in, the better.'

Brian nodded, and headed out. Liz suspected he was quite relieved to be away from Constance's vandalism.

'There!' Constance separated Lady Henrietta from her frame, took a pair of cotton gloves from her pocket and put them on before taking the canvas out fully. She examined the edges that had previously been hidden, with her eyeglass and torch.

Outside, the fracas was rising to a crescendo. As well as the frantic barking, Liz could hear James Bullington shouting, and Lukasz yelling gleefully.

'RUN, NELSON, RUN! DON'T LET HIM CATCH YOU!'

After what seemed like an agonizing length of time but was probably only a few minutes, Constance straightened up.

'Okay,' she said. She started to put the Reynolds back into the frame.

'Okay?' echoed Liz. *What did that mean, for heaven's sake?*

Infuriatingly, Constance ignored her.

Gryzna prompted. 'Is it a fake?'

'Not now.' Constance was frowning with concentration.

'But...'

'Shut up and let me do this.'

Constance's urgency seemed to be justified. The noise outside was subsiding. When Bullington's voice came again, it sounded very close.

'IF I SEE THAT DOG ANYWHERE NEAR HERE AGAIN – EITHER OF THOSE DOGS NEAR HERE – I'M CALLING THE POLICE.'

Liz and Gryzna exchanged an anxious look. Was Bullington coming back?

'There,' muttered Constance. The painting was exactly as it had been, framed and intact. She gave the tools back to Liz just as the door started to open.

'Gloves!' hissed Liz. Constance stripped off her gloves and rammed them back into her pocket just in time. Too late, Liz realised there was no way she was going to be able to get out. For a second, she froze, like a rabbit in the headlights, but then Gryzna pushed her towards the counter. She ducked behind it.

Luckily, as James Bullington came in, all his attention was on the dog panting in his arms.

'There, there, Mr Dandy. Did those brutes try to hurt you?'

Crouching behind the counter, Liz stifled a protest. It had been Mr Dandy chasing Nelson, not the other way around.

'Shall I take him?' suggested Brian. 'I'll give him some water.' Liz heard the internal door open and close as he took the pekinese into the utility room.

'I'm so sorry for that interruption,' said James smoothly to Gryzna. 'Where were we?'

'We seemed to have come to something of an impasse,' said Gryzna. 'I am not prepared to buy the picture without proper examination, and a proper examination involves taking it out of the frame.'

'As I said, I am happy to do that, but only if you pay a deposit of two thousand pounds. A gesture of good faith.'

'You will deduct that from the sale price?'

'Naturally.'

'And what if my father decides not to buy the painting?'

'That's up to him, of course. But the deposit stays with me. Small change, I would imagine, for a person of your father's calibre.'

Gryzna deliberated.

'One thousand,' she said, at last. She seemed to have forgotten this wasn't for real – her competitive business sense had taken over. Liz stifled her impatience. They'd done what they came to do. She just wanted to get out of there.

Bullington hesitated. 'Make it one and a half, and we have a deal.'

'One thousand two hundred. Please email your bank details and I will make the arrangements.'

Gryzna and Constance took their leave, with lots of hand-shaking and protestations of good faith. To Liz, crouched under the counter, it seemed to take forever. Eventually the door *bing-bonged* as they exited.

'Well,' said Bullington to Brian when they'd gone, 'I have to say I'm surprised at Connie Threadwell, getting mixed up with people like that. Still. We shouldn't look a gift horse in the mouth, I suppose. We'll both be getting a juicy commission.'

'I should think so.' Brian stepped behind the counter. He glanced down, and his eyes met Liz's. They widened. He jerked his attention back up to Bullington and stepped away again.

'You know, I think Mr Dandy might have hurt his paw. I think he was limping when I put him in the utility room.'

'Limping?' Bullington sounded horrified.

'Just a bit. Perhaps he's pulled a muscle, with all that running about? Do you think we should take a look at it?'

As soon as she heard the internal door open and close again, Liz scrambled out of her hiding place and legged it out the door. She ran across the grass to the shelter, where everyone else was waiting.

'Bloody hell! We thought you were a goner there,' said Niall.

'What happened?' asked Skipper.

'IS IT A FAKE OR NOT?'

'I have no idea.' Liz, breathless, bent to hug Nelson, who was looking extremely pleased with himself, tongue lolling. 'We'll have to ask Constance.'

23

'Genuine? Are you sure?'

Constance eyed Liz sourly. 'I've been at Sotheby's for twenty years. I trained in Florence and also spent three years at the Sorbonne, doing my PhD in eighteenth century portraiture – of course I'm sure. The painting in the gallery is a bona-fide Reynolds.' She tutted. 'That will teach me, I suppose, for getting dragged into a wild goose chase.'

'I don't understand.' Liz was crestfallen. 'I was so sure it was a fake.'

Everyone else in the café was silent, gutted that the theatrics at the gallery had been for nothing.

'So what happened to the other horse portrait?' asked Skipper.

'Wherever it is,' said Constance, 'it isn't under Lady Henrietta Cholmley.'

'What now?' Gryzna folded her arms.

'I suppose we just have to let the law take its course.' Liz was bitterly disappointed. She was still pretty sure that

Christian had discovered something he shouldn't have, and that it wasn't Stevenson who had killed him. But now she had no idea what was really going on.

Constance retrieved her suitcase from behind the counter. 'I need to get back to York.' She spoke to Gryzna. 'I'll pick up the dress and jewellery another time.'

'I'll drive you to the station,' said Dickie.

The café door opened with a tinkle. Benedict stepped in, and stopped in his tracks when he saw everyone.

'Hello,' he said, surprised. He took in Tilly and Mags, Iris and Dickie, Niall, Liz, Skipper and Griff, Nelson, Gryzna, and the boys, who were stuffing their faces with hotdogs at one of the tables. 'What's everyone doing here?' He spotted Constance. 'Con? I thought you were in London.' His eyes slid to Liz. 'What's going on?'

'AND YOU NEVER THOUGHT TO MENTION ANY of this to me?' Benedict's tone was mild but Liz could tell he was hurt. Angry, even. Two spots of colour burned in his cheeks.

'Excuse me,' said Skipper. 'I have to get on.' He nodded to Benedict. 'Good to meet you, at last. See you later, Liz. Come on, Griff.' Griff trotted out after his master.

Constance had already left to catch her train, whisked off by Iris and Dickie. Niall stood, awkward.

'Me too. See you back at the cottage, Mrs M.'

Mags and Tilly and Gryzna disappeared tactfully through the curtain into the kitchen, leaving Liz and Benedict alone. The boys were still eating, oblivious to anything other than food.

Benedict lifted an eyebrow. He still hadn't had an answer to his question.

'I didn't want to bother you with it.'

'Bother me?'

'I know how busy you are.'

Benedict said nothing.

Liz glanced at the boys. 'Let's take this outside, shall we?'

THEY WENT OUT, and, by unspoken accord, cut down the side of Sandgate onto the pebbly beach. Liz slipped Nelson off his lead, and he ran off to investigate a lump of seaweed.

'I thought we were a team,' said Benedict.

'We were. We are.'

'So why didn't you tell me what was going on?'

Liz found she had no answer, other than the truth. 'I thought you wouldn't approve.'

'Really? What on earth would make you think that?' She realised he was being ironic.

'There's no need to be snippy.'

'I can't believe you thought that...' he struggled to find the right word, '...ridiculous performance was a good idea.'

'We all did.'

'Then you're all as bad as each other. Although I expected better of Con.'

Liz bristled. 'Constance is a big girl. She has a mind of her own.'

Benedict caught her tone. His expression shuttered, and he said nothing.

'This isn't really about what happened today, is it?' prompted Liz.

'What do you mean? '

'Something isn't right. It hasn't been right for a couple of months. Ever since that business on the *Stella Mae*.'

'I take it Skipper was involved in that?'

'He was, yes.'

Benedict said nothing, just looked deep into her eyes, as if searching for the answer to some unvoiced question.

Something nudged her leg. Nelson had brought her a piece of driftwood. She bent to take it from him, and when she straightened up again she saw Benedict's expression had changed. He'd come to a decision.

'I think we should take a break.'

She was half expecting it, but it still felt like a punch to the stomach. 'Really?'

'Let's give each other some breathing space.'

Now it was Liz's turn to be silent. She felt tears prickle her eyes and turned away to throw the driftwood for Nelson. She blinked her tears away, not wanting Benedict to see them. When she turned back, she hoped they'd gone.

'If that's what you want,' she said.

'Isn't it what you want?'

'No. I don't think it is. '

But Benedict had seen her hesitation. 'Let's just give each other some space for a while.' He dug his hands into his pockets. 'See how it goes.'

Liz shrugged. 'Okay.' She couldn't trust herself to say anything more.

He held her gaze for another few seconds, then nodded, before turning and crunching away over the pebbles. Liz watched him go, a tall figure hunched against an imaginary wind. She had an ache in her throat. She tried to swallow it, but it was lodged there like a stone.

She felt another nudge on her leg. Nelson, with his driftwood. She took it from him.

'Come on, sweetie. Let's go home.'

. . .

WHEN SHE GOT BACK to Gull Cottage, Niall's blue eyes searched her face.

'The kettle's just boiled, if you want a cuppa,' he said gently.

'I'm fine.' She hesitated. 'Actually, I might just go to bed.' She glanced at the clock on the kitchen wall. It was only half past eight, but she didn't care. 'Can you give Nelson his night-time walk?'

'Sure. No problem.'

Liz headed up the stairs. Niall called after her, 'I'm going to make you that cup of tea anyway. I'll bring it up.'

She took off her make-up in the bathroom, trying to ignore her splotched complexion and reddened eyes, and trying not to think too much. Then she fled to the sanctuary of her bedroom. She got into her pyjamas and, leaving her clothes in a heap on the floor, burrowed into bed.

It had been so easy for Benedict to suggest they take a break, and that had really hurt her. They'd been so good together, only a few months before. Where had it gone wrong?

There was a knock on the bedroom door. It was Niall, carrying a tray with tea, a sandwich, and a couple of chocolate digestives.

'I thought you might be hungry,' he said.

'Thanks. I'm not, really. But thanks anyway.'

'I'll leave it here, just in case.' He put the tray on her dresser, and peered at her anxiously. 'Are you okay?'

'I'm fine. Honestly.'

She saw his sceptical look.

'It's nothing a good night's sleep can't sort out. Don't worry about it.'

He nodded and went out. Liz went back to bed.

Benedict's unspoken implication had been that Skipper had something to do with the estrangement between them, which was outrageous. It was much more likely that Constance was the source of the problem. Benedict had been spending so much time with her.

Liz sighed. If that was the case, if he was attracted to Constance, there wasn't much she could do about it, was there? But it was going to be really hard. Whitby was a small place, and they had the same circle of friends. It would be difficult, seeing him around and not being able to touch him. Or kiss him.

She pulled the duvet over her head. This wasn't the worst day of her life – she'd had many more dreadful ones when Mark was dying.

But she still wanted it to be over.

24

L iz woke to the sound of more summer rain pattering on the roof window of her bedroom. In spite of her emotional turmoil, she'd slept heavily. Now she just felt numb.

The bell in St Mary's Church on the cliff above her chimed the hour. Six o'clock. She knew she had another hour or so before Nelson would want his walk. She snuggled under the duvet.

How would Benedict feel this morning, she wondered. Relieved? Or would he regret their break-up? She sighed, and pushed the thought out of her mind. She would just exhaust herself with imaginings. Instead, she tried to distract herself by pondering the fiasco with the painting. That had been humiliating too – she'd been so sure the Reynolds was a fake. How could she get it so badly wrong? Of course, it would be a terrible gamble for Bullington to risk selling a fake in his gallery. It could ruin his reputation. She'd been naïve. If James Bullington wanted to sell a fake painting, he would probably be much more underhand about it.

Liz sat up. Of course he would.

Oliver Edwards had run the story in the *Bugle*, about the painting being stolen. He'd said some of the national papers had picked it up. Was it possible that James Bullington had deliberately fed that lie to Oliver's young reporter, knowing it would spread? Had he done it to make a black market sale seem legitimate?

Liz swung her legs out of bed.

The walk to Spring Hill was a wet one. By the time she arrived at the police station her legs and feet were soaked, and there was rain dripping off her waterproof hat. Inside, the waiting room was quiet, with only one lone member of the public and his dog.

PC Williams looked up from the counter behind the screen as he heard her come in. His long face broke into a smile.

'Mrs Mac. How are you? If it's DC Ossett you're looking for, he's still off sick, I'm afraid.'

Liz smiled at Williams, glad Kevin and Anna were getting to spend some much-needed time together. 'Actually, Bill, it's you I was hoping to see.'

'WHAT IF HE DENIES EVERYTHING?' said PC Williams half an hour later, as he was driving them to the gallery in one of the squad cars. Liz had explained everything to him at the station.

'I imagine he probably will,' said Liz. 'But isn't it worth taking the chance to try to flush him out? We really have nothing to lose.'

'*You* have nothing to lose. Flint will have my head on a spike if she hears about it. How do we know Bullington won't make a complaint?'

'He'll only do that if he's innocent. And then at least we'll know, won't we?' She saw his uncertain expression. 'If you've changed your mind, it's okay. We don't have to do it.'

PC Williams shook his head. 'No. I want to. I have my NIE in a few months' time. It can't hurt to show some initiative.'

'NIE?'

'National Investigators Exam. If I get a good enough pass, I might be promoted to detective.'

'You'll make a great one.'

'Thanks. You're the only one who thinks so. I've been getting so much grief about it at the station, I haven't told anyone I'm taking the exam.'

It only took a couple of minutes to get to the West Cliff. Unable to find a parking space on the promenade, Williams parked on the grass right in front of the gallery. A policeman's perk.

James Bullington was on his own when they went in – there was no sign of Brian or Mr Dandy, and no visitors in the gallery. He looked up when he heard the door, and glowered at Liz. His scowl deepened when he saw she was dripping rainwater onto his marble floor. Then he spotted Williams, and his face smoothed.

'Officer, what can I do for you?'

'I have a few questions, if you don't mind? Is there somewhere private we can go?'

'We can do it here, if you like. We're hardly rushed off our feet.' Bullington led them to seats at a table beside some metal sculptures on plinths. The sculptures, that were abstract but vaguely horse-like, hadn't been there for the party. As Liz sat down, Bullington gave her a questioning look, clearly wondering what on earth she was doing there. Williams coughed, nervous. Liz gave him a reassuring nod.

'We've been looking into the time discrepancy between Christian Petit's death and the burglary. Our suspect, Mr Stevenson, claims he had locked Mr Petit in the upstairs bathroom when he left, around two-thirty.'

'I'm not sure–'

Williams didn't let him finish. 'We've found some evidence that Christian Petit was a blackmailer.' He blushed at the lie. It was only half a lie, really – Liz was pretty sure Christian had been blackmailing Bullington, but there was no actual evidence to prove it.

'Good heavens!' Bullington's surprise seemed real. 'Who was he blackmailing?'

Williams hesitated. 'You.'

'Me?' Bullington gaped at him.

Williams plunged valiantly on. 'We know you've been selling fake paintings on the black market. We believe you also used the break-in as an opportunity to kill Mr Petit and frame Mr Stevenson. Two birds with one stone, so to speak.'

'Are you completely out of your mind?'

'We believe you hit Mr Petit, viciously and without provocation, at the top of the stairs.'

'And when exactly am I supposed to have done that?'

'When you let him out of the bathroom. After you opened the gallery.'

'That's a fine theory. There's only one problem – I didn't open the gallery.'

Liz and Williams stared at him.

'Brian opened the gallery that morning.'

'Brian?' Williams frowned.

'He opens the gallery every morning.'

'But you were here when we arrived. You told us you found the body together.'

Bullington looked uncomfortable. 'I suppose that wasn't strictly true. Brian found Mr Petit, and called me when he called you. I only live in Hudson Street, two minutes away.'

Williams stared at Bullington in disbelief, but Liz wasn't really surprised that Bullington had lied about finding the body. He was such a narcissist. He'd clearly bent the truth in order to be at the centre of the drama.

They heard a muffled growl. They all turned and saw that Brian was standing beside the door, with Mr Dandy on his lead. They hadn't heard him come in. Liz had no idea how long he'd been there.

Williams found his voice. 'Is this true? Were you the first on the scene?'

Brian unclipped Mr Dandy. 'I was. It was me who found Mr Petit. And I promise you he was very, very dead. I should think it was the fall that killed him – that limp of his, probably, that tripped him up coming down the stairs.'

Williams shook his head. 'Mr Petit had a wound on the back of his head that was inconsistent with a fall. The coroner thinks he was already dead when he went over the banister.' He looked at Liz for confirmation.

But Liz only had eyes for Brian. 'I thought you said you'd never met Christian.'

'What?'

'When Niall and I spoke to you in the Copper Kettle. You said you'd never met him, because you were on holiday when he started working here... How did you know he had a limp?'

Brian frowned. 'I don't know.' The young gallery assistant

looked flustered, suddenly. Everyone was staring at him. He shrugged. 'I must have heard it somewhere, I suppose.'

But he could read the disbelief in their eyes.

'Whatever.' With that one word, Brian let his mask drop. Gone was the affable expression, the helpful demeanor, replaced by something quite different: malice. 'Don't blame me.' He pointed at Bullington. 'Blame your bloody sisters. If they hadn't cooked up that ridiculous scheme of theirs, everything would have just kept ticking along with Dennis as usual.'

'Did you kill Dennis too?' asked Liz.

Brian gave her a frosty glare. 'What's it got to do with you?'

Liz stared at him.

'No, seriously,' he continued. 'That's a genuine question. Because none of this really has anything to do with you, does it? Someone should teach you to mind your own bloody business!'

Brian made a dash towards Liz, and before anyone could move, he'd toppled her backwards off her chair. His hands went round her throat. She felt the pressure, and clawed at him, but couldn't pull his hands away.

'Mind... your... own... bloody... business.' Each word was punctuated by a vicious shake.

Stars burst behind her eyelids. She couldn't breathe! Pain exploded, as her head was slammed into the floor. Just as darkness threatened to swallow her, she heard a crash, and then a groan. They came from a long way away.

She felt the pressure go off her. Then everything went black.

25

'**B**RAVO!'
Everyone clapped as the players took their bow on stage. Niall – sweaty and red faced now he'd taken his Smaug head off – grinned at his friends, who made up a good portion of the audience.

Tilly whistled. Kevin stamped. Mags, Iris and Dickie, Kevin and Anna all cheered and clapped. Gryzna, Skipper and Benedict hadn't made it to the performance. Gryzna had the boys to look after, and Skipper was out on the *Stella Mae*. Benedict had a meeting in Middlesbrough, but had promised to join them in the White Horse and Griffin when they got back to Whitby. Liz wasn't sure if she was happy about that or not. It had been two weeks since their break-up, and she hadn't seen him yet. Their regular Mahjong nights had been cancelled, ostensibly because everyone was busy but really because it would be too awkward for everyone involved. After Brian's attack, she had half expected Benedict would call her, but he hadn't. That had hurt more than she cared to admit.

'THAT WASN'T HALF BAD, WAS IT?' shouted Iris in Liz's ear.

'No, it was very good.' What the students lacked in acting skills – they were still learning, after all – they'd more than made up for with enthusiasm. Niall had been particularly good as Smaug. Although they hadn't been able to see his face, his voice had been suitably sinister and thrilling.

When the players went off stage, everyone made their way to the café of the community college to wait for Niall.

'How's your throat?' asked Anna.

'Not too bad, thanks.' Liz's voice was still raspy. She'd been released from hospital only a couple of hours after Brian's attack. She wouldn't have been so lucky if Bill Williams hadn't used one of the metal horse-like sculptures to whack Brian over the head. Brian's skull had fared better than the sculpture, but it had still given Williams enough time to prise Brian off Liz and overpower him. Unfortunately for Williams, however, the sculpture had been expensive, which rather diminished his status – in Flint's eyes at least – as hero of the hour.

'You could do with some arnica cream for the bruising,' said Anna. 'I think I have some at home. I'll drop it off for you tomorrow.'

'Thanks.' Liz touched her throat. She had a lovely necklace of blue fingerprints, now ripening to black and yellow – to remind her of the lessons she'd learned.

It had turned out her intuition wasn't as infallible as she'd thought – at least as far as people were concerned. She had genuinely liked Brian, thinking him uncomplicated and friendly, but she couldn't have been more wrong. Niall's instincts had been much nearer the mark, but she hadn't listened to his warning. Liz resolved she would listen to her friends in future, and she'd be much more careful about putting herself in harm's way. Brian had come very close to killing her.

Kevin joined them. 'Everything okay? Dickie's taking orders for coffees if you want one.' Anna gave Kevin a peck on the cheek and went to the counter to join the others.

Liz wasn't worried about coffee. It was still something of an effort to eat and drink.

'Guess what?' said Kevin. 'We found Lady Henrietta's twin sister today. In a lockup Brian was renting at Sandsend.'

'So I was right; there was another one?'

Kevin nodded. 'Brian had been using Dennis to make forensic copies of some of the paintings at the gallery. He's been selling them to online buyers abroad, using fake provenance and authentication. Our tech guys have gone through Brian's emails. He had a buyer lined up for the Reynolds in Colombia. We think he was waiting until the original had been sold before shipping the fake.'

'Do we know how Christian found out about it?'

'We're not entirely sure, but we think Dennis told him. Probably when he was drunk.'

Liz nodded. Juliette had told her that Christian and Dennis had been drinking buddies. A thought occurred to her. 'Do you think that's why Christian took the job at the gallery? Do you think he saw it as an opportunity?'

Kevin looked thoughtful. 'It's possible. He was definitely blackmailing Brian. We've found evidence on Brian's phone.'

'Brian's still denying killing him, though?'

''Fraid so.' Kevin pulled a wry face. 'And Dennis. We think we have him, though. We collected touch DNA – epithelials – at both scenes. We're just waiting for the results.'

Liz was silent for a moment, wondering what might have happened if Angel and Skye hadn't put the opportunity in Brian's way to get rid of Christian. Would Brian have kept paying Christian to keep quiet? Or would he eventually have decided to kill him anyway? It was anybody's guess. With Dennis, however, things were a little clearer. When Christian was murdered, Dennis must have realised what had happened. Brian simply couldn't risk him getting cold feet and telling someone.

Liz's thoughts were interrupted by the appearance of Niall, his neck and hands still green with stage paint.

'Well, what did you think?' he demanded.

'Excellent!'

'NOT HALF BAD. '

Tilly and Mags clapped. 'Well done.'

Niall beamed at them all. 'I'm gagging for a beer. Let's get back to Whitby.'

THE WHITE HORSE and Griffin was already busy when they piled inside half an hour later. All the seats were taken in the narrow, panelled bar, so they had to stand. No one seemed particularly bothered by it.

'What can I get you to drink, Mrs Mac?' called Niall.

'A gin and tonic, please,' rasped Liz. She hoped the alcohol would numb her throat. And her nerves. She'd scanned the bar for Benedict as soon as they arrived, but he wasn't there yet. She didn't know if she was looking forward to seeing him, or dreading it.

When they all had their drinks, Niall lifted his beer in a salute.

'Cheers!'

'CHEERS!'

'To dragons!'

'To dragons!'

Liz saw the warm look that passed between Mags and Tilly, and remembered the plush Welsh dragon that had been taken to Benedict's house. A gift from Mags to Tilly, that had since returned home to roost. Kevin put his arm around Anna's waist and hugged her. Dickie and Iris clinked their glasses together. It was all very convivial and cosy.

The door opened.

'B!' yelled Tilly. 'Over here.'

Benedict grinned. He could hardly miss them in the tiny bar. His eyes scanned the group, and found Liz's. His smile flickered, but stayed. A universal smile, meant for all. He joined them.

'Sorry I couldn't make it,' he said. 'How did it go?'

'Great,' said Niall. 'Everyone remembered their lines. And I was fabulous, wasn't I?'

'YOU WERE. YOU GAVE BENEDICT CUMBER-SNATCH A RUN FOR HIS MONEY.'

'I wish I'd seen it. Is there another performance?'

'No, there was only one, for our end of year.'

'That's a shame.' Benedict clapped Niall on the back, and pointed at his already empty glass. 'What are you having? Let me get you a refill.'

Liz looked at Benedict, surrounded by friends, laughing and congenial. She couldn't believe how quickly they'd gone from strangers, to friends, to lovers and back to... what, exactly? Friends? She didn't think so. There would always be a reserve between them now. Strangers, then. Acquaintances, at best.

Tilly caught her eye, and grimaced in sympathy. Liz

raised her glass to her, and emptied it in one painful swallow.

'I think I might head home,' she said, quietly so no one else could hear.

'Already? Are you sure?'

Liz nodded. 'Nelson's been on his own for too long. He'll need a pee. Will you make my excuses to everyone?' She didn't want to make a big performance of leaving.

'Of course.' Tilly pecked her on the cheek. Liz slipped out of the door without anyone else noticing.

She walked home, heartsore, through the quiet cobbled streets. The air was warm, and fresh from recent rain, laced with the scents of seaweed and salt. A few herring gulls still circled overhead, even though it was after ten o'clock. It would be midsummer soon – the longest day. The sky wasn't dark, but tinged with pink, pearled with light. Liz looked up at it and felt the balm of nature spreading through her, soothing her pain. She let her mind roam free.

Somewhat to her surprise, it landed on Skipper. What was he doing at that moment, she wondered, out on the wild North Sea? Was he also looking up, watching the light leave the sky?

Was he thinking of her?

AUTHOR'S NOTE

Whitby is, of course, a real place – a jewel of a town nestled on the North Yorkshire coast, on the edge of the North York Moors National Park. It's a popular tourist destination, most famous for being the birthplace of Colonial explorer Captain Cook, and the inspiration for Bram Stoker's Gothic masterpiece *Dracula*. I've done my best to keep Whitby's geography – its street names and layout – as close to the real thing as possible.

The White Horse and Griffin Hotel is real. So is the Brunswick Centre, The Captain Cook Memorial Museum, the Magpie Café and the Duke of York pub, where Niall works. And, of course, the Abbey and St Mary's Church continue to attract visitors from all over the world. I have tried to describe them as accurately as possible.

Kipper Cottage and Gull Cottage are based on the two cottages closest to Fortune's Smokehouse, on Henrietta Street. The Anchorage Retirement Home, the Full Moon

Café and the Copper Kettle Café are my own inventions, although Sandgate, where the Full Moon is located, is always popular. It's packed with fascinating little shops, including the Whitby Glass workshop, where they make the town's famous Lucky Ducks.

The village of Robin Hood's Bay is about six miles North of Whitby, and is well worth a visit. If you don't have a car you can get the x93 bus from Victoria Square in Whitby, and it will get you there in about twenty minutes. Of course, If you're feeling energetic, you can walk it, along the coastal path – a section of the Cleveland Way. It's a gorgeous walk, but quite steep in places. It should take you about three hours, depending on how fit you are and whether you stop to smell the roses.

How Robin Hood's Bay got its name is something of a mystery – it's highly unlikely Robin Hood ever visited North Yorkshire (or even that he actually existed). But some local legends claim that Robin Hood thwarted an attack by French pirates who pillaged the village. He returned the loot to the people.

Marnar Dale House doesn't exist, as far as I know. I named it after the second beck that runs down into the village, in addition to King's Beck.

Boosbeck Hall is also fictional, a loose amalgamation of National Trust stately homes I've visited. For any of you who aren't based in the UK, the National Trust is England's much-loved charitable body responsible for protecting historical sites. They do a tremendous amount of great work preserving the UK's heritage, and were responsible for saving many large houses bequeathed to them when the families that owned them were no longer able to pay for their upkeep. You can become a National Trust member, which gives you reduced entry into their properties, and helps the Trust continue their work. National Trust properties are also well known for their brilliant cafes and home baking – there's even a book, *The National Trust Book of Afternoon Tea,* available on Amazon.

Talking of home baking, I highly recommend The Cornish Bakery on Church Street in Whitby, where Tilly bought her celebratory cheesecake. I'm not sure they actually sell cheesecake, but I'm particularly fond of their almond croissants and *pastel de nata* for breakfast. There's usually a queue waiting when their doors open in the morning.

I hope you've enjoyed this latest instalment of the Kipper Cottage mysteries, and that you'll join Liz and her friends again.

Until then, happy armchair sleuthing!

If you'd care to leave a review on Amazon they are enormously helpful in getting books discovered by new readers and I would be grateful for you thoughts.

ABOUT THE AUTHOR

Jan lives just outside Edinburgh with her husband, three kids, a one-eye whippet and a fat black pug. Born in a colliery village in the North East of England, she cut her literary teeth on the great storytellers of the 60's and 70's - Wilbur Smith, Frank Yerby, Mary Renault, and Sergeanne Golon. She began her writing career as an advertising copywriter, and has since had novels published by Random House and HarperCollins, and original audio series produced by Audible UK. She also writes for tv.

Jan enjoys psychological thrillers and crime fiction of all kinds, from the coziest of cozies to the blackest of noirs.

You can find Jan at www.kippercottagemysteries.co.uk

ALSO BY JAN DURHAM

Kipper Cottage Mysteries

Death at the Abbey (Book 1)

Death at Neptune Yard (Book 2)

Death at the Feast (Book 3)

Death at the Anchorage (Book 4)

Death on the Stella Mae (Book 5)

Death on the West Cliff (Book 6)